CH00855405

Zara's Folly

CLARE REVELL

ZARA'S FOLLY

Choices Consequences and Responsibilities Book 1

Scripture taken from THE HOLY BIBLE, NEW INTERNATIONAL VERSION® NIV® Copyright © 1973, 1978, 1984, 2011 by International Bible Society®. Used by permission. All rights reserved worldwide.

Cover photo by Trudi Eisner with Jess © Trudi Eisner 2017
Image ID : 5235192 purchased from 123rf.com © Jos Alfonso De Tomas Gargantilla
Cover design by Marion Ueckermann © Marion Ueckermann
Horse scene breaks © Katie Hawkes

ISBN: 1548501131
ISBN-13: 978-1548501136

DEDICATION

For Ralph and all the other JAC horses.

Dear Reader,

I had a blast writing this story. It just got longer and longer and took on a mind of its own. Don't you just love it when that happens?

We all make choices every day, what to wear, what to eat, whether to snap back at someone or smile sweetly and ignore them. What isn't important so much isn't the actual choice; rather it's how we deal with what follows. We all mess up. Even Christians mess up. God created us with free will, the freedom to make our own decisions. But we have to stand by those choices and deal with whatever the fall out or repercussions are. We don't get a real life 'get out of jail free card' even if we think we deserve one.

The stables I based Hebron on really exist. Called Rehoboth, they are run by Just Around the Corner (JAC) Ltd a UK Berkshire based registered charity committed to engaging with young people and their families, enabling them to make positive choices, by demonstrating love and acceptance according to Christian principles.

Their website is here - http://jacoutreach.org/cm/

A portion of the royalties from the sale of this book will be going to them.

And I promise no actual horses were harmed in the writing of this book.

ACKNOWLEDGMENTS

This book would not have been possible without help from the following people.

Jess Revell for being a fount of all things horse related and letting me bug her day and night with questions – some of which had obvious answers. I just had brain-freeze at the time. She is also responsible for naming the hero, the horses, as well as the stable hands.

My cover models - Jess and Blue.

The people at JAC for allowing me to base the stables on theirs, for letting me use Jess and Blue as the cover models.

Naomi Milligan for answering a shed load of questions on the running of the stables, vets and farriers.

Katie Hawkes for drawing the amazing horse I used for all the scene breaks.

National Rail Enquiries for routes between York and Reading.

Jan, Marion and Angela for their editing skills.

Whatever happens, conduct yourselves in a manner worthy of the gospel of Christ. Then, whether I come and see you or only hear about you in my absence, I will know that you stand firm in the one Spirit, striving together as one for the faith of the gospel without being frightened in any way by those who oppose you.
Philippians 1: 27-28a

CHAPTER 1

ZARA MICHAELS RAN DOWN THE STAIRS to the platform, praying the train wouldn't leave before she boarded it. The guard was closing the doors as she reached the train. "Wait," she called.

He turned and held the last door open long enough for her to plunk her case inside and climb in after it. "Have a good trip, miss."

"Thank you."

Somehow she stowed her case and rucksack in the one remaining space on the luggage rack. The automatic doors to the main carriage hissed open. Zara made her way down the already swaying carriage in search of her seat. She'd almost missed the train, thanks to her sister Kim's incessant meddling, not to mention yet another lecture from her father.

One blessing in disguise. At least her forward facing seat was empty. These days not even a reserved sign guaranteed that. And the way the day was going she'd expected to find someone already sitting there.

She regarded the old lady in the aisle seat and managed a faint smile. "Excuse me. May I get past you, please?"

"Of course, dear." The old lady stood to allow Zara access to her seat.

"Thank you." Zara suddenly teetered into her seat as the train jolted over the junction points to the main line. She put her handbag on her lap, squashing it between the table and her middle. She turned to the window, pushing her glasses up her nose as the train sped up. The houses and factories of York slid by, becoming sparser before turning into fields and trees as the city was left behind.

Zara focused on the window, the trees and forests, fields and streams zipping by. Faster and faster, *clickety-clack*, the train sped through the English countryside—relentlessly taking her into pastures unknown, but at the same time along a path she knew all too well.

"Tickets, please, ladies and gents."

Zara pulled her ticket from her bag, along with the reservation card and held them out to the conductor. He glanced at them and nodded as he handed them back. Zara returned them to her purse. Her phone beeped and she sighed. The photo of Jordan was obscured by a message that read Kim Mob.

Can't you leave me alone for an hour, sis? What do

you want now?

The message made her heart sink lower. *ARE YOU REALLY GOING TO DO THIS? AUNT AGATHA LOVES THAT PLACE. TELL DAD NO MORE. SO WHAT IF HE DISINHERITS YOU B/C YOU WANT A LIFE OF YOUR OWN AND DON'T WANT TO DO HIS DIRTY WORK ANYMORE? IS THE MONEY REALLY MORE IMPORTANT?*

Another text quickly followed.

ARE YOU THERE? YOU MADE A COMMITMENT TO CHRIST, ZA. YOU CAN'T GO BACK ON THAT AND COMPROMISE YOUR SOUL.

Then a third message.

CALL ME. OR AT LEAST PROMISE ME YOU KNOW WHAT YOU'RE DOING. AND MAKE SURE YOU CALL JORDAN EVERY NIGHT.

Zara scowled. "Course I will," she muttered. "I'd hardly go away and not call, now would I?" She shoved the offensive phone to the bottom of her bag. "Now try bothering me."

The old lady cocked her head and stared at her. "Are you all right, dear?"

"Yeah. Tired of my phone beeping."

"My son is always on his phone. He wants me to have one, but I don't see the need. I'm too old for this face thing or the non-stop chirping. And you miss out on so much with your head constantly peering down at a tiny screen."

"I know what you mean." Zara settled back in her seat, and crossed her ankles. "Kim, my sister, is permanently attached to hers. I really wish I'd left mine

3

at home. I only use it for calls and texts, nothing else. It's what she calls a thick phone."

"Thick?"

The bloke opposite chuckled over his book.

"Not smart like hers. Oh, I can access the internet, email, take photos and so on, but I have a computer at home for that. I don't need it on my phone as well."

As the old lady rattled on about her son, grandchildren and the weather, Zara studied the man seated opposite her while replying. He was kind of cute with short, slightly wavy dark hair. His dark eyes flitted across the pages, his full lips pursed, his long tanned fingers holding the book almost reverently. Oh, there was something sexy about a man who read. Her gaze slid across his broad shoulders, and down the tanned muscular arms his shirt sleeves didn't hide. The tan indicated he either lived abroad or worked outside. Going on appearance alone, he was definitely her type.

Finally the old lady beside her stopped chatting and fell asleep.

Zara sighed with relief. Then whispered a prayer of apology. She should be grateful anyone took the time to speak with her without recognizing her and asking for an autograph.

The bloke opposite stood. "Could you watch my things for me for five minutes or so, please?"

"Sure." Zara tried to ignore the goose bumps the sound of his chocolaty-smooth voice raised. She watched him stride down the swaying carriage. Once he was out of sight, she grabbed his book. Taking care not to lose his place, she read the back cover. It sounded interesting and she made a mental note of the title. A historical thriller set during the last war. Exactly the sort of thing *she* loved to dive into and get lost inside. She laid the book back down, making sure to place it exactly how she'd found it.

Tucking her hair behind her ears, she wished she'd thought to have packed something to read, but she'd left in such a rush, she was amazed she'd packed a suitcase for herself. Jordan's things took up so much more room than her own. All she had in her handbag was a notebook, pen and coin purse. And the phone she hated with a passion. Her Bible and puzzle book were in the case. No way was she unpacking that on a crowded train. Knowing her luck, a pair of her knickers would tumble to the floor. Or worse, that black lace bra she loved so much.

She'd left the laptop at home, having closed all her social media accounts that morning. She needed a complete break from everyone and everything—Jordan being the exception, but that was different. Yes, she was still reluctantly working for her father—one last job. She was tired of the way he ran his business and what he expected her to do. She really was tired of helping her father get richer than he already was by scamming their property out of the poor fools.

She'd become more and more uncomfortable with that aspect of the job and becoming a Christian made it impossible. She found herself having to compromise more and more, until she reached breaking point.

The only way out was to break free. The hold her father had over her, made that impossible. Losing her inheritance didn't bother her. But Jordan…

Kim called it folly. Zara would rather call it… Honestly? She didn't know what she called it. It wasn't running away. Reality check maybe? A new beginning? The Lord knew how much she needed one. How much she longed to run away and start over. Somewhere. Anywhere. She wanted someone to accept her, along with her past and the baggage she came with.

She heaved a sigh. That wasn't going to happen any time soon. At least not one that was good enough for her father to approve of the relationship.

No, she had to leave. If turning her back on everything in York made her broke so be it. Once this was over, that was it.

Done. Dusted. Finito.

Perhaps Aunt Agatha would help—or at least have an idea of what to do.

Snoring resounded in her left ear, and then the old lady snorted, shifted in her seat and settled down again. The scent of coffee floated through the carriage. At that moment there was nothing in the world Zara wanted more than an infusion of hot coffee. Preferably a large strong one. But there was no chance of that for a while— at least not until her seat mate woke. Did this train even have a buffet car? For all she knew, the aroma could be coming from someone who might have thought ahead and included a thermos flask with their packed lunch.

The cute bloke reappeared with a cup in each hand. "I

thought you might like a coffee." A bright smile lit his face. He plonked down the take away cups and slid one across the table. "I could see you weren't able to get out and it seemed mean to drink in front of you."

She returned his smile. "Thank you. I'm dying of thirst."

"Good job they have plastic lids. I nearly came a cropper on that last set of points."

"That could have been messy."

"You're telling me." He reached into his pockets, pulled out several sachets of sugar and creamer and a couple of stirrers. "Almost as messy as dying in your seat from thirst."

She tilted her head and held out a hand. "Well, not literally dying. I'm Zara."

"TJ." His firm warm grip encompassed her hand for far too short a moment as he slid back into his seat.

"How much do I owe you?"

"Nothing. Call it a thank you for diverting our sleeping friend from talking *my* ear off."

Zara gently removed the lid from her cup and inhaled deep of the enticing scent. She ripped open the sugar, tipping one sachet after the next into the hot liquid. "Honestly, I wasn't really listening. Just nodded and responded in the appropriate places." She added creamer, stirred, and replaced the lid. She sipped, burning liquid scalding its way down her throat.

The train began to slow as it approached Sheffield. The old lady woke, gathered her things and headed to the end of the carriage.

Zara glanced after her. "Bye, then," she said quietly.

TJ snorted. "My brother does that. Along with shouting 'thank you' when motorists don't give way at crossings. Or 'you're welcome' when he does something for someone and doesn't get a thank you in return. One of these days he's gonna get thumped for doing it." He set his coffee on the table. "It was a good idea of yours to reserve a seat. I thought I was going to have to stand all the way home before I found this one."

"It was the only train going direct," she explained. "Well kind of. I have to change once if my aunt can't collect me. Some of the trains meant changing three or four times, plus a tube trip. I hate the underground with its closed in spaces."

"Me too. You going far?"

"Reading, to stay with my aunt."

"Holiday?"

She shifted and hid behind her paper cup for a few seconds. "Kind of. What about you?"

"Back to work. I've been staying with my brother in Scotland for a few days. Trying to persuade him not to sell his half of the business we co-own." He swigged the coffee. "It didn't work."

"Can you buy him out?"

TJ gave a short, bitter laugh. "I wish. But there's no way. Someone is coming to value the place on Monday, but even without that valuation I know I can't afford a mortgage. Sides, we inherited the place together when Dad died." He wrinkled his nose. "But you don't want to hear all that."

Zara's phone beeped. "Excuse me." She picked it up as TJ went back to his book. The screen read Aunt Agatha.

OF COURSE I WILL PICK YOU UP AT READING. SAVES CHANGING TRAINS AND GETTING THE ONE TO EARLEY. I'LL MEET YOU ON THE MAIN CONCOURSE. THEY'VE DONE AWAY WITH PLATFORM TICKETS. SOMETHING TO DO WITH CRACKING DOWN ON PEOPLE RIDING TRAINS WITHOUT PAYING. THEORY BEING WITHOUT A TICKET YOU CAN'T GET ON THE TRAIN OR PLATFORM. STUPID IDEA IF YOU ASK ME. IF YOU REALLY WANT TO JUMP A TRAIN YOU'D FIND A WAY, PLATFORM TICKET OR NO.

Zara grinned. *YUP. LOOKING FORWARD TO SEEING YOU. TRAIN GETS IN AROUND HALF PAST FOUR.* She tucked the phone away and glanced across at TJ. He was engrossed in his book. Zara leaned against the back of the seat and drained her coffee. Then she closed her eyes. Time for forty winks instead of worrying about the task ahead.

TJ Greggson wasn't reading so much as staring at a jumble of words on a page. He could read—well kind of—but a full-blown novel was beyond his meagre capabilities. Especially the way the words jumped off the page and danced all over the place. Xavier knew reading was an issue for TJ, which was why things worked so well between them. Xavier did the admin, the paperwork, book-keeping, and the management side of the stables. TJ dealt with the animals, children, and practical stuff.

His stomach rebelled against the bitter coffee. He actually preferred tea, but the railway tea was undrinkable and so weak the joke was if his face was that colour his mother would sit up with him all night. Mind you, if Alicia made the tea at work the same thing applied.

There was no way he could run the stables on his own. No way would the bank loan him the millions needed. Maybe millions was an overestimate on his part. Irrespective of hundreds, thousands or millions, any self-respecting bank would turn him down flat in a heartbeat with his credit rating.

He turned a page, keeping up the pretence of reading. Over the top of his book he glanced at Zara. She'd seemed impressed by the fact he was reading a book not a paper if the glances she'd initially given him were anything to go by. He wasn't going to disillusion a pretty girl like her. Silky blonde hair cascaded over her shoulders, blue eyes now closed as she slept, glasses sliding down her nose. Her hands clutched her bag, left ring finger empty; although why that mattered he wasn't sure. It wasn't as if he was going to see her again after the train stopped in Reading.

And even if he did, she wouldn't be interested in a bloke like him.

According to his brother, no sensible girl would ever be. TJ knew different. He didn't amount to nothing. He was someone. Alone maybe, but someone. God knew who he was and had a plan for him, like it said in Jeremiah twenty-nine. Pastor Morgan had preached on that the other week.

The only problem would be walking in the desert for seventy years first. He wasn't looking forward to that, but he guessed he was at least part way through that now. Or maybe that's where he was headed. About to lose his home and job all in one foul swoop because Xavier wanted to move to Scotland to be a crofter on some remote island way off the coast. Well, technically he already had moved and in TJ's opinion, needed his head examined. The place was so remote it was virtually uninhabited. There were a total of thirty people, if that, on the entire island.

He still wasn't sure why his brother wanted to do this. He'd stopped listening after a while, instead trying to convince him to stay at the stables. He shouldn't have done that. He slid his phone from his pocket and scrolled to his brother's photo before hitting the green button. "Hey, it's me."

"You can't tell me you're home already." Xavier laughed. "I didn't think they'd invented transporters yet."

"Only car ones. No, we've just passed Sheffield. I wanted to apologize for leaving the way I did. I never gave you the chance to talk or explain properly."

His brother chuckled. "That's you all over, TJ. Are you sure you're ready to hear my point of view now?"

"I can always hang up on you. Go for it."

"Like I showed you, it's a small beef croft. I'm renting to start with, but I've been given the option to buy, hence needing to sell my half of the stables. I can grow veg to sell at the market, here and on the mainland. They also want me to teach at the local school. There are only six kids right now, but their only other option would be lessons on the radio and that doesn't always work."

"Teach? You?"

"I used to, remember? Okay, this is slightly different as the kids are all different ages and will be in the same class, but it's a good thing, TJ. This is the opportunity of a lifetime. I can make a difference there. I can't pass it up."

TJ scowled at the window. "What about me?" Yes, he knew that was selfish, but if he didn't think about himself, no one would.

"To be blunt, bro, you're twenty-six. It's time you stepped up to the plate and did something for yourself. Go back to school. Take those classes."

"With what?" TJ sighed. "Where do I live? You sell and I have no home, no job and no way to pay for those classes you insist on. No bank will touch me without any qualifications, will they?" The train rattled over the tracks. TJ grabbed his cup just before it slid into his lap. Then grabbed Zara's as it slid across the table towards him. At least hers was empty. "I better go. I'll text you when I get in."

He hung up and glanced over the table. Zara was still sleeping and he was grateful he hadn't been overheard.

He shoved the book into his rucksack and retrieved his headphones. Plugging them in, he turned to the window. The countryside raced past. *I hope you have a plan to rescue me, Lord, because right now I'm drowning.*

He pulled up the Bible app on his phone and settled back to listen. He didn't need to read, because the app read to him.

Before he realized it, the view from the window became familiar. He removed his headphones and tucked them back into his rucksack. The phone returned to his pocket as the driver announced the next stop as Reading.

Zara woke with a start. She checked her bag and stood, making her way to the end of the carriage.

TJ pushed to his feet, and followed her to the end of the carriage. He'd left his case in the luggage rack there. Tugging his case free, he set it near his feet.

"Thanks again for the coffee." Her smile made a rotten day a whole lot brighter.

"You're welcome." The train stopped and TJ opened the door. "Let me help. Normally I'd say ladies first, but this would be easier." He jumped down to the platform and lifted the bags and cases from the train one by one, before offering Zara a hand.

A thrill shot through him as she grabbed his hand, her cool touch setting his nerves alight with…just what he couldn't say, but something good.

All too soon, she let go and retrieved her case and rucksack. "Thank you. Bye."

He stood there, like an idiot, watching her vanish into the crowd. Then he shook his head, shouldered his rucksack, pulled up the handle on his case, and strode toward the main concourse.

Zara was ahead of him and he paused, seeing her hug Agatha Michaels, someone he knew from church. Could Zara be Agatha's niece? It was a small world after all.

He headed past them to find a taxi.

"TJ?"

He turned. "Hello, Agatha. Zara, we meet again."

"You already know my niece?" Agatha's face was a wonderful mix of confusion, astonishment, and the "you stole my thunder" look.

"We sat opposite each other on the train from York." He shifted his rucksack strap back up to his shoulder.

"Ah. Are you going straight home?"

"That's the plan. Once I find a taxi, that is."

Agatha shook her head. "Nonsense. I'm going past your door anyway. Zara wants to see the local area, and there's no time like the present."

TJ shot a sideways glance at Zara, who hung her head and shifted uncomfortably. "Well," he began.

Agatha cut him off with her usual aplomb. "Good, that's settled. Come on then." She grabbed his case in one hand, Zara's in the other, leaving the two of them in her wake.

"I'd hoped she'd changed," Zara said. "But I guess not."

TJ laughed. "That's the Agatha we all know and love. But you wouldn't really change her, would you?"

She shook her head. "No."

Agatha turned. "Come on, slow coaches. I don't want

to go over my time on the car. Costs a small fortune to park here. Daylight robbery if you ask me."

TJ gestured with one hand. "After you." He fell into step beside Zara, following Agatha to the car park.

Zara slid in the front of the car, quiet as a church mouse, while Agatha and TJ chatted. She watched the trees and houses slip past as her aunt drove from the town out into the country. It really didn't take long, despite the size of Reading, to hit the green and yellow fields of farmland—wheat crops rippling in the breeze.

After half an hour, during which she hoped her aunt wasn't matchmaking while she wasn't listening, the car stopped. Zara gazed out at the huge barns and stables. Black wrought iron gates set in a smart red brick frontage bore the name *Hebron*.

Shock resonated. Her nerves vibrated the way guitar strings hold the note long after they're plucked. Aunt Agatha had told her about the charity work this place did—with disabled and disadvantaged kids, along with mainstream riding and hacking or pony-trekking. All of the staff or the majority of them were Christians. Even the name Hebron came from the Bible. It was one of the six cities of refuge that kept scared men alive.

TJ opened the car door. "Thanks for the lift. I'll grab my gear from the boot." He got out and went around the back of the vehicle. The boot opened and closed.

Aunt Agatha swung around in the wide entrance way.

Zara sucked in a deep breath. "I don't believe this. You know why I'm here, right?"

"I assumed a holiday. I'd expected you to bring Jordan; you're inseparable most of the time."

She shook her head. "I'm working. It wouldn't be fair on Jordan, so he's staying at the *hig bouse with Gampa* as he puts it. Dad wants me to check out the land. He wants to buy it, level the whole area and build houses."

Aunt Agatha slammed on the brakes. "What?"

Zara felt heat rush to her face. "Don't shoot the messenger. The place is being sold. Dad wants me to check it out."

Her aunt scowled and began driving again.

"TJ was saying on the train that he can't afford to buy his brother's half of the business they co-own. I hadn't realized it was this place."

"I didn't know Xavier was leaving."

"Left from what I gather. TJ was staying in Scotland with him trying to get him to change his mind. I've already told Dad this is the last time I'm doing his dirty work for him. I'm tired of it. This place cements my decision. I can't do this anymore."

"Does TJ know why you're here?"

"No. And you're not to tell him."

"I've already booked the hack for you for Monday, like you asked. Although I now wish I hadn't." Aunt Agatha sighed. "If I'd known this was your plan all along…"

"That's why I didn't tell you. As if things weren't

bad enough already. No matter which way this goes, one of us is going to end up out of work and living on the streets." She caught the sideways glance her aunt gave her. "It'll most likely be me anyway. Dad made it abundantly clear what'll happen if I defy him—homeless, jobless, and disinherited. But I've had enough. Once this is over, I'm out. The only problem is Jordan."

"Speaking of Jordan, what did you tell him?"

Zara sighed. "That I had to go away for work. I hate leaving him, which is why I'm quitting. I just need to find a way to do it."

Aunt Agatha nodded. "That explains the text I got from Kim. Something about talking Zara out of her folly."

Zara snorted. "Not possible. I need to get Jordan out of that house and safe. Being here for a few weeks will give me the space I need to come up with a plan."

CHAPTER 2

EARLY MONDAY MORNING, TJ sat in the office, his head buried in his hands. He hadn't slept much the night before. All the good of the Sunday services had evaporated the instant he returned to the stables. How many more days did he have left here before the home he loved was sold? He glanced out of the window at the old house which stood to one side of the yard. The first building anyone saw when driving in.

His grandfather had built that house and the original stable block. That had been replaced five years ago with a state of the art building after the American fashion of parallel rows of horse stalls. TJ's father had been raised here. As had TJ himself. He loved being able to hear the horses "gossip" as Nanna had called them from the bedroom—even more so now they could see each other. And in the summer when the horses were in the field all night, he could still hear them. They were his friends. He couldn't sell them any more than he could sell his own soul.

In front of him on the desk lay the books and paperwork the estate agent had requested. Also the information for this financial adviser the bank was sending out. TJ rubbed his hands over his face. "Why is my brother selling, Lord?" he groaned. "I can't do anything else. I don't want to do anything else. I'm not clever like him. I struggle over basic things. The only thing I'm good at is horses."

Slowly, the yard came to life as the stable hands arrived for work. TJ leaned back in his chair. What would happen to the horses if the new owner only wanted the land? He'd have to lay off the staff. It wasn't merely his life they were talking about here. It was several—both animal and human. Something else his brother had conveniently forgotten.

TJ rose and headed out into the morning sunshine. He breathed in deep of the smell he loved so much. A combination of hay, horses, even the ever present muck heap meant home. Salt stung his eyes and he blinked rapidly. Shaking his head, he moved into the stable block. Each horse had their head down, feeding contentedly. All apart from Celeste who, as always, was throwing a hissy fit.

He strode to the end stable and grabbed the feed bucket from Gerry. "She's been like this all night. I'll see to her." Moving to the stable door, he glared at the horse. "Back."

Celeste ignored him, shaking her head and whinnying.

"Back!" TJ yelled. He smacked the bucket on the door, before dropping it over the side. At least it landed upright this time. The mare glared at him, then stepped away and lowered her head over the food. TJ shook his head. "You are one bad tempered, moody mare, aren't you?"

Alicia came over to him. "Hey, boss. Ready for today's list?"

TJ peered at the brunette beside him. Alicia was his right-hand woman when it came to running the stable side of things. "Go for it." He followed her back into the office and over to the chart on the wall. The chart was divided into columns with photos of the staff along the top instead of names. Between the two of them they had designed a system that worked.

Aside from his brother, Alicia was the only other person who knew his secret.

Alicia pointed as she spoke. "As always, yellow are sessions with horses. Green are the classes. Your meetings are in red. One before lunch and one afterwards. You have a hack in orange. Agatha Michaels rang and booked it while you were away. It's not for her, but someone she knows."

TJ laughed. "I couldn't imagine Agatha on a horse, no matter how hard I tried." Maybe it was Zara. He'd hoped to see her again, but she hadn't been in church yesterday, even though Agatha was. Running his finger along his column, he checked off his list. "Okay. We have craft class, hack, meeting, lunch, and meeting. What's this purple one?"

Alicia giggled. "Your turn to poo pick."

TJ roared with laughter. "So long as it isn't purple poo, I'm there. I can't afford the vet this week. In between this lot I have to find time to mow the field so we can put the horses in it tonight. There's more shade there. So don't use it if you can avoid it this afternoon."

"I can take the hack if you like. Although Miss Michaels did ask specifically for you."

"In that case, I'll do it. We'll go up the road, across the edge of the downs and back. Should take about an hour or just over."

"Who do you want tacked up and I'll make sure they're ready at ten?"

"I'll take Tog. Tack up Rumple. He loves hacking and is the least likely of all of them to spook out on the road."

"Famous last words."

The clock on the office wall chimed. TJ shoved his hands into his pockets. "Okay, time to get on. Who do I have this morning?"

"Craft with Marty and David. The paint is out ready along with pots, sticks, and tissue paper. Although I have no idea what you're making."

"Marty told me it's his mum's birthday, so we're making flowers in pots. It'll be brilliant, you'll see."

He headed out into the small classroom in the main building where the boys were waiting. The hour's craft making flowers sped by, both children fully engrossed. It was a shame they couldn't cope in a school environment, but seemed to be thriving in the few sessions they had here a week. He'd hoped to be able to expand their education, but that didn't seem like it would happen now. Not if Xavier sold him out.

Val arrived to take the boys for maths. TJ grinned as they both showed off their flower pots, before heading into the bathroom to wash up.

He glanced down at his shirt. Washing up himself would probably be a good idea. As he passed the office, the bell on the gate rang and he pressed the button to open the gate. The car was Agatha's. Presumably she was here to drop off whoever she'd booked the horse for.

He held his breath waiting to see who got out. His heart pounded as Zara exited the vehicle, jodhpurs clinging to her shapely figure, hat in her hand. The paint covering him was forgotten as he strode to the door to greet her.

Agatha waved, and then did a three-point turn. The gates opened automatically to let the car back out onto the main road.

TJ smiled and held out a hand. "Hello, again."

"Hi." Zara ran her eyes over him. "I have a hack booked."

"I was hoping it was you. Alicia said Agatha had booked a ride for someone while I was away. Have you much experience with horses?"

She angled her head. "You're covered in paint. And you have some here." She pointed to her right cheek and then to her shirt.

22

"I've been doing a craft session. I was on my way to clean up when you arrived. Come on through. I won't be a moment."

TJ led her into the office and grabbed a clean shirt from his locker. He had paint all over his jodhpurs as well, but they could stay dirty. He strode to the sink in the corner of the room. While it filled with hot water, he pulled off his shirt, tossing it to the side. "You didn't answer my question. Do you have much riding experience?"

"A fair bit." Zara sounded distracted.

"Like what?"

"I can jump, gallop…" Her voice trailed off.

TJ glanced up. She was watching him in the mirror. Her cheeks pinked up, and she lowered her gaze. He smirked and grabbed the soap. "Gallop?"

"Uh…gallop, hack. I play polo, sometimes. I have my own horse."

"Nice. What sort?"

"A cob. His name is Pipkin. He's seventeen hands. We keep him in a stable near where we live."

"Have you done any eventing?"

She shifted uneasily. "Some."

He studied her in the mirror as he dried off. She was hiding something. The question was what. He hung the towel up and emptied the sink. Grabbing the clean shirt, he tugged it over his head, before turning around to face her. His shirt bore the name of the stables on one side and his name on the other. "Then let's see what you can do. Stable rules say you have to do a fifteen minute riding check in the school first."

She baulked. "I just told you what I can do."

"And I could say I can jump higher than a lamppost, but unless I can prove it, words aren't good enough."

Zara snorted. "Anyone can jump higher than a lamppost."

He grinned. "Aye, 'cos lampposts can't jump. You heard that one then?"

"My sister's favourite joke."

TJ grabbed his hat and riding gloves from the desk. "Let's go."

"You're taking me?" Surprise filled her eyes.

"Another rule. I'm the boss. I do the first of everything. Kind of a hands-on boss."

"I thought you co-owned your business. At least that's what you said on the train."

He shrugged. "Xavier, when he was here, did the paperwork, books, admin stuff. So why he's jacking all this in to be a crofter in Scotland I have no idea. He hates the outdoors."

"Crofter?"

TJ strode to the stable block. "It's a kind of land-tenure and small holding in Scotland. Mini-farm if you like. Very traditional up in the highlands and islands. He grows crops and animals, teaches—or he will do—in the local school. Anyway, this is the stable block."

"Wow. It's huge."

"We expanded just over five years ago. The original building with one long row was replaced with this. Two rows facing each other. We have nine horses, with room for three more. Alongside this, we have the school—both covered and open—three fields, and a small menagerie which includes ducks, goats, chickens, rabbits, and guinea pigs."

"And your brother left this to run a farm?" Amusement tinged her voice, matching the glint in her eye.

"I know. Stupid, right?" TJ gestured to the far side of the yard. "Over there we have classrooms and the office block."

"What's that building by the gate?"

"That's my home. It's a lot safer for the horses if someone lives on site and it's the way it's always been done. My grandfather built this place from nothing. My father grew up here. I grew up here. There's a lot of history here and Xavier's—"

TJ broke off and sucked in a long deep breath. "And you don't want to hear any of this." He strode across to the two tacked-up horses standing by the fence inside the outdoor school. "This is Rumple. He's fifteen, pretty good natured, and steady."

Zara patted Rumple's neck. "He's lovely. Shire-cross-draught if I'm not mistaken. And named after Rumplestiltskin, I assume?"

TJ nodded. "Rumple for short. This one is my own horse." He patted the white Cob. "Her name is Tog." He handed Zara a florescent yellow high-vis jacket. "These are non-negotiable for riding anywhere outside the stable grounds."

She slid into it. "Rightly so."

He admired the way Zara mounted smoothly, taking time to whisper to Rumple and settle him as she did so.

He patted his horse. "I'll be back for you in a few minutes, Tog, and then we'll go out. You'll like that, huh?"

Tog nuzzled him and whinnied.

Zara chuckled. "They talk back, huh? Maybe you could give me a tour, time permitting?"

TJ nodded. "Okay. Off you go." He leaned against the fence and put Zara through her paces. The fifteen minutes became five, as it was easily apparent she knew what she was doing. There was something inherently familiar about the way she rode, her bearing in the saddle. She knew far more about riding than she was letting on. Even her name seemed vaguely familiar. And he knew he wasn't getting her confused with Princess Anne's daughter, even though she was an equestrian.

"Okay, let's go." He untied Tog and opened the gate to allow Zara through. He led Tog after her, and then closed the gate. Mounting his horse, he nodded to the main gate. "We have to watch the road out of here. It's not usually busy, but being country, people drive like idiots and ignore the speed limit. Or ignore the triangle warning signs that say horses use the road."

"That's not only confined to country folk," Zara drawled in a spot-on-perfect country accent. "Them city slickers can be just as stupid ya know."

He glanced sideways at her, admiring her profile. She sure knew how to sit on a horse. "So how do my stables compare to the ones back home?"

"These are much bigger, not to mention cleaner. The horses seem happy."

"Most of them." TJ settled into his saddle as Tog settled into her stride. The summer breeze was a welcome relief from the heat of the morning. He loved hacking or jumping or merely riding around the school. He and Tog made a good pair.

"Oh?"

"There's always one isn't there? Like that one kid at school who ruins it for all the others and causes class detentions."

"Like me you mean? I never did learn how not to answer back in class."

He smiled awkwardly, having meant himself. "There's one horse here. She's a rescue horse, but enough said about that."

"Sounds like a story there."

TJ turned off the road, taking the path that led up over the downs. "Kind of. Xavier never could resist a sob story."

"You must be shorthanded with him gone."

"Tell me about it. I'm expected to be in two places at once, and it's not possible."

"I can help out a little if you like. I'm around for a month or so. Maybe longer, it depends."

He cocked his head, shooting her a curious glance. "How can you take that much time off work?"

Zara didn't meet his gaze. "I just can. But the offer's there."

"I can't pay you. Not if you're already in paid

27

employment."

She nodded. "That's fine. Call it voluntary. I love horses, and I'm pretty good at paperwork."

TJ laughed. "I can't do paperwork to save my life. Xavier did that. To say I struggle with it is an understatement."

"Then let me help. I can muck out, lunge or whatever you need and keep the books in order. I'd like to. I have to leave by four today as I'm due at the garage to pick up my hire vehicle."

"Thank you. I'll drive you over there myself." The phone in his jacket pocket rang. He scowled. "Excuse me." He pulled his horse ahead of hers. "Hello."

"Sorry boss," Alicia said. "The estate agent is early and he'll only talk to you."

"Okay, give me ten minutes to get back." He snapped the phone shut and turned Zara. "Sorry. This bloke turned up early for the meeting and I have to get back. I promise we'll go out another time."

Zara raised an eyebrow, sending it vanishing under her hat. "I'll take you up on that offer."

TJ paused, and then realized what he'd said. "I… yeah, okay." He turned Tog and headed back down the path. "If you're sure about volunteering and you can start today, I can put you to work immediately."

"That's fine. Sounds good."

They clattered through the gates and into the yard.

Alicia strode out to greet them and grasped Tog's bridle. "I really am sorry, boss."

TJ jumped down. "Can't be helped, I guess. This is

Zara. She's going to volunteer around here for the next wee while."

"Oh?"

He removed his helmet and gave her his trademark stare.

"I mean, sure, boss."

"Good. Show her the ropes and put her to work. I'll need her in the office at two. She's a whizz at paperwork apparently, which is just as well since you and I are hopeless."

Zara dismounted as TJ trudged across the yard toward the offices. Anyone would think that the weight of the world had suddenly descended on his shoulders. She tore her gaze away and glanced at Alicia. She held out a hand. "Zara Michaels."

The woman shook her hand. "Alicia Smith. You certainly made an impression." Alicia clicked her tongue, leading Tog across the courtyard to the fence. She tied her to the ring. "I didn't even know he was hiring."

Zara tied Rumple the same way. "He wasn't exactly. He said he was short staffed. I offered to help as I know horses and paperwork. Just tell me what I need to do, and I'll do it."

Alicia glanced at her, face impassive.

"What?"

"This is so not TJ."

Zara shrugged. "He knows my aunt. We got talking on Friday on the train from York. He seems like a nice bloke."

"He is. Okay. Right now, the horses are inside since they were out last night. Most of them are sleeping. These two need to be checked over, sponged down to cool them off, and groomed. Then they can go in their stalls—all the doors are marked with the horse's names. The mucking out was done first thing, but we still need to poo pick the field and a dozen other jobs. The other horses will need exercising today. Aside from Pogle. It's his rest day. TJ insists all the horses get one day off a week, to kick back and relax."

Zara patted Rumple's neck. "We do that as well— sounds like a good idea."

"And if you're staying for a while, I'll need to take your photo for the board in the office. You may have noticed that TJ is dyslexic, so we have both a visual and colour system in the office. That way he knows what's going on. All the staff here know, but no one mentions it. It's kind of an open secret. I'll show you once his meeting is done." She grinned. "He also has a pretty good memory, he just can't read very well."

Shocked, Zara did her best to hide it. He hadn't been reading that book at all? "He does a good job of concealing it."

Alicia nodded. "He does. He can read a bit, but not much. Okay, I'll get these two some water, if you could take the saddles off them. The tack room is to your right.

30

All the pegs are labelled. Leave your hat on any time you're around the horses."

"Same as at home." Zara removed the saddles and bridles, whilst Alicia put buckets of water in front of the thirsty horses.

Alicia handed her a brush. "This one is Rumple's. There's tepid water and a sponge there for him." She glanced up as TJ yelled her name across the yard. "That's my cue. Better go see what he needs me to read now."

Zara nodded. She squeezed out the sponge and assessed Rumple. "Okay, boy. You know how this goes, right? And yes, I have done this before. Loads of times." She sighed. "Pipkin would love it here. So would Jordan. He loves horses, like I do."

She began sponging down Rumple. Could she ever get back into this line of work? She wouldn't have to ride or compete. There was no way the team would have her back. And even if they did, she didn't want that again. Her medals were tucked away safely. No one here, it seemed, recognized her and that suited her fine.

TJ leaned against the wall, watching as the estate agent drove out of the gates. Then he returned to his office and slammed the door, before sinking into his chair and burying his head in his hands. He'd asked Alicia to join them and confirm the figures, not wanting to believe what the estate agent was telling him. His worst fears had come to pass. The land his father and grandfather had built on and made to thrive, and then bequeathed to both him and Xavier as joint owners, was worth in excess of half a million. Twelve acres of land, animals, buildings, equipment. Even half of that was way out of his price bracket, never mind all of it.

Admittedly with his half share, he could buy a small house somewhere outright. But then he'd also need to find a job.

He groaned, fingers digging into the sides of his head. Grief tugged at his very soul. *Who am I kidding, Lord? No one would employ me. I can't read. I can't count. The only thing I know is horses and I can't go from owner to stableman. You may be working all this out for good as it says in Romans, but can't my good come into this somewhere, not just Xavier's? 'Cos right now, he wins and I lose.*

His mobile phone rang. TJ snatched it up. "Hebron. TJ Greggson speaking."

"Hey, bro." Xavier sounded even chirpier than normal.

TJ scowled, his mood blackening further. "What do you want?"

"Well that's nice. What's up?"

"You know very well what's up. The estate agent left a short time ago." He pushed to his feet and shoved the papers across the desk, watching them fall like confetti to the floor. He stormed outside, slamming the office door behind him. "You want to know what he said?"

"I know what he said. I've just got off the phone with him."

"Then you know I can't afford—"

"I told him to put the place on the market for the full asking price. I've given him a reserve at which he can accept the offer."

Anger replaced the grief and frustration. TJ narrowed his eyes. "You. Did. What?" he yelled. "How could you?"

"Only a small part of that money would buy the freehold up here. It would get you a house outright. It would put Dad's legacy to use and—"

"Shut up! Dad's legacy *is* this place." He hung up and hurled the phone across the yard into the muck heap.

"Nice shot!" came the cry across the yard. Gerry gave him a thumbs-up. "Just don't expect me to retrieve it."

"It can stay there," TJ replied. He stomped across the yard and leaned against the stable wall.

Zara regarded him from where she topped up the water buckets, blue eyes twinkling behind her glasses. "Bad morning?"

"The worst." He sighed. "Did Alicia show you how to put the beds down?"

She nodded. "The one behind you is done. She's lunging Pippin, so I made the most of it. Mucked out his stable and freshened it."

He glanced behind him. "Perfect. Thank you."

"There's a horse in the back that is still inside. She isn't at all happy. Did you want her turned out?"

"That's Celeste, the rescue horse. She's never happy

and hates going outside. But yeah, I'll get her out, and then we can clean her stable." He headed into the end stall and grabbed Celeste's halter.

Celeste stood in front of the door, glaring at him. She huffed and pawed the ground with her left front leg.

"Don't you give me that," TJ told her firmly. "I am in no mood for you today. You are going outside for a few minutes."

"What's wrong with her?"

"Just bad tempered." TJ put the halter on. Celeste tried to shake it off. "Pack it in."

"I didn't do anything," Zara protested.

"Not you, the horse. She's unridable, bites, kicks, stamps. Xavier rescued her to avoid her being put down."

"How long has she been here?"

TJ manoeuvred the stubborn animal to the door. "Two weeks. As long as my brother's been gone."

Zara set down the broom and moved to his side. She took hold of the other side of the halter. "Come on, girl," she said softly. "Let's go enjoy this lovely sunny day for a few minutes. It's meant to be wet tomorrow."

Celeste whinnied and shook her head.

"Come on." TJ pulled on the halter. "You may not want to go out, but I am not cleaning out your stable with you in it."

They managed to get the horse outside and into the field. Celeste stood there, pawing the ground, putting weight on three of her four legs.

"She favours that front right leg, see?" Zara pointed

to it.

"She was lame when we got her. Waste of money if you ask me. Can't do anything with her, even if she'd let you."

Zara's phone rang. She ignored it.

"You not going to answer that?"

"I'm working. Besides, everyone has personalized ring tones and I really don't want to speak to my father right now."

"You didn't leave it on the train then?"

"Oh, sometimes I wish I had." She tugged the phone from her pocket and turned it off. "There. What's next?"

"Celeste's stable."

"Sure thing." Zara headed back inside.

TJ stared across the field. He wasn't ready to say goodbye to all this. There must be something he could do. If only he knew what.

Shortly after four, Zara bade farewell to TJ as he dropped her off at the garage. She collected the motorbike she'd hired and drove back to her aunt's house. She wheeled the bike down the side path and locked it in the garage.

"I'm back," she called. "I'm going to change and I'll be down."

"Okay. Dinner's almost done."

Five minutes later, Zara entered the kitchen. She

inhaled deeply. Minced beef if she wasn't mistaken. Hopefully cottage pie or maybe even mince and roast potatoes. "Something smells good."

"Glad to hear it." Her aunt beamed. "How was your day?"

"It was good."

"Your dad rang. Said you weren't answering your phone."

"I didn't want to speak to him. 'Sides, I knew if it was urgent or about Jordan, he'd tell you and then you'd call me. TJ is a nice bloke. He doesn't deserve what's happening. He actually offered me a job at the stables. That's where I've been all day."

"I figured as much. But you already have a job."

"One I don't like or enjoy." Zara plunked the carton of juice on the table. "This one is voluntary. And I love it."

"I can tell. You look happier than you've been for a long time."

Zara dropped into a chair. "I don't miss competing. I do miss the horses. Getting down to see Pipkin once a month isn't the same as being around him all day, every day. TJ doesn't know how blessed he is." She paused. "Well maybe he does. He's been in a foul mood most of the day since the estate agent came over."

Aunt Agatha said grace.

Zara picked up her fork. "You know what I do. Dad sends me places he wants to buy. I have dinner with the owners, convince them to sell to Dad at a lower price to get a quick sale to prevent whatever dirt Dad has on them from coming to light. I hate it. I hate what I've become because of it. And I'm not convinced it's as legal as he says it is. Dad's made a huge amount of money out of this over the years."

Her aunt paled. "He's what?"

"He's a pirate, basically. At first, I didn't see anything wrong with it. I mean it paid for me to get ahead in riding. But there were rumours he bought my place on the team. I'm sure they're not true, but they're still there. Since I gave my life to Christ last year, I've been questioning a lot of Dad's motives. His work ethic and so on. It's become harder and harder to work for him. I'd quit in a heartbeat if it weren't for his hold over me." She brightened. "And the stables? You should see them."

"I have."

"They are amazing. So much space. And the horses seem so happy and well cared for."

"Anyway, your dad left a message for you. He said to remind you that you work for him and to keep in mind the consequences of failing." Aunt Agatha worried her bottom lip. "I don't like the sound of that."

Zara put the fork down, no longer hungry. "I see. One mistake and he's going to hold it over me forever."

Aunt Agatha frowned. "You can't call Jordan a mistake."

"No. Jordan is never that. Dad will never forgive me no matter what I do. I'm tired of all the lies. No more. God gave me a new start. It's time Dad did as well."

"What are you going to do?"

"I don't know. But things are going to change."

"Good. Now eat before I feed you. Horses are hard work, and you need to keep your strength up." She paused. "Maybe I can get Jordan to come and stay here as well."

Zara snatched up the fork again, shoving it through the mince. "Dad won't let him out of his sight. He won't even let me speak to him until I've been here a week and made progress. It's like I'm twelve and grounded again. I have to find a way to get us both safe. I just don't know how yet."

Her mind flew back to TJ. He didn't need the added problem of her father either. She'd watched him struggle with the paperwork that afternoon. It wasn't dyslexia, at least not the ordinary kind. It had to be something more. The way he'd described the words jumping off the page and blurring made her think there was something else going on, and part of her was surprised the teachers at school hadn't picked up on it years ago. She'd have to research later.

But right now, she needed to eat before Aunt Agatha really did feed her. She took a small mouthful. "Do you really think you can get Jordan out of that house?"

Her aunt nodded. "Leave your dad to me. It may take a few days, but I'll think of something. And I'm not letting you go to bed tonight without speaking to him either."

She grimaced. "Dad or Jordan?"

Aunt Agatha winked. "Eat or it won't be either of them. You think your dad is bad. Wait 'til you see what happens when *I* ground you."

CHAPTER 3

ZARA PUT HER FORK DOWN. "That was lovely, thank you."

Aunt Agatha smiled. "Good. Now it's time for you to call Jordan."

"I told you, Dad won't—"

"Ack." Her aunt cut her off. "Leave that brother of mine to me." She grabbed her iPad and hit the video call button, making sure Zara was out of shot.

The dialling tone rang and rang before being replaced by her father's voice. "Agatha, this isn't the best time."

"Hello to you too, Jamie. I want to speak to Jordan. He must be missing Zara."

"He is, and he's acting up."

"All the more reason for me to calm him down and read to him."

"He's in bed, in disgrace. I don't want Zara…"

Aunt Agatha hissed. "You put Jordan on here right now, or I'll see to it that Zara is on the first train home." She glanced up at Zara across the table and raised an eyebrow. "I might even drive her myself."

"Fine."

Aunt Agatha turned to Zara and whispered, "He's paused the camera." She nodded to the kitchen worktop. "On the bread bin, in the paper bag, you'll find a copy of his favourite book. You can read to him."

Zara beamed. "Thank you." She stood and went to retrieve the book. As she picked it up, Jordan's voice rang from the iPad behind her.

"Auntie Aggie!"

"Hi, Jordan. Is Grandpa still in the room?"

"No. He gave me this, and then went away. He's cross."

"I've got someone who wants to talk to you." She handed Zara the iPad.

Three-year-old Jordan beamed, bouncing up and down in sheer delight. "Mummy!"

"Hey, bug." Zara sat down and cradled the tablet in her hands. "Mummy misses you."

"I miss you, too. When you coming home?"

"A couple of weeks."

"But that will wait ages." Jordan's face fell.

Zara's heart clenched with sorrow. "I'm know, baby, and I'm sorry. But Mummy has to work. I promise this is the last time I'm ever going away and leaving you."

"Can't I stay with Auntie Aggie, too? I don't like it

here. Gampa is cross all the time."

"I'll see what I can do. See, what I got?" She held up the anthology of stories. "Auntie Aggie bought it 'specially so I can read to you."

"Can I have the star story?" Jordan held up his copy.

Zara chuckled. "It's not Christmas, but okay." She flipped to the last story. "It was Christmas in Tannoch. Angus the airship had watched as the townsfolk had begun to decorate the houses and streets."

As she read, Zara's resolve grew. Things had to change. The time had come for the world to know Jordan was her son, not her brother. She'd fought to have him, fought to keep him. The struggle had cost her so much. Her career, her place on the British team, and most of all, her self-respect.

She was almost at the end of the story, when Jordan's eyes fluttered shut. Experience told her he'd be properly asleep in two minutes. Zara touched the screen gently. "'Night, Jordan-bug. I love you."

"Love you, Mummy…" he whispered.

Zara carried on reading. Then she put the book down. "I can't do this…"

Aunt Agatha held out a hand. "Give me the tablet, dear, before your dad comes in."

Zara took a last look at her son, and then pressed the red button to end the call. "I miss him so much it hurts. I have to fight for him."

"Is the birth certificate in your name?"

She nodded. "Yes. And he knows he's mine. Dad simply won't admit it in public."

"Easy done then. I'll insist he comes here to stay for a few days. I'll tell Jamie it'll help you work better."

Zara snorted. "I'm volunteering at the stables…"

"I'm sure I can find a few parks to visit with him during the day. And we can all go riding. He'd love to see the horses. Then we can also find you somewhere to live. A long way away from your dad."

"He won't like it."

"Tough. He can't have everything. He's had you under his thumb for long enough." Aunt Agatha reached over the table and grasped Zara's hand. "In fact, you could both live here with me for the time being. It would be fun. And I'd like the company."

Zara's vision misted. She blinked furiously. Her aunt had been the one person who'd stood by her. Who'd known the truth about Daniel, Jordan's father. "I should have stayed with you after I had Jordan. Not gone back home."

Aunt Agatha squeezed Zara's hand. "We both know you didn't have a choice. But now you do. Did you hire a car?"

"Motorbike."

Her aunt rolled her eyes. "And how are you going to ferry a child around on that?"

"I'll change it once he's here." She searched her aunt's eyes. "Can we really do this?"

"Yes. Give me a few days to work on my brother. We need an iron clad plan he can't disturb."

Bitterness twisted Zara's heart further. "You mean destroy."

Aunt Agatha grinned. "That too. You know I get my words muddled."

"So you want the dishes in the washing machine, yeah?"

Her aunt shook her head. "Go on with you."

Zara rose. "I'll do them. You put your feet up for a bit."

"Thank you, dear. That'll make a nice change."

"While you're sitting there, can you search something up for me online? Colour dyslexia. I was going to do it, but maybe between the two of us, this madcap idea I have will make sense."

"Sounds intriguing."

Zara stood and picked up the plates. "Hopefully it'll help someone, but I need to check out a few things first."

The next morning, TJ stared at Celeste, returning the same evil eye she was dishing out. "Don't you give me that look. It's about time you learned how things are done around here, missy." He tried to put the head collar on, no easy feat with the way she was tossing and whinnying. He scowled. "Pack it in. I can't muck out your stable with you in it." *Not without risking serious injury.*

"She still doesn't want to go out then?"

TJ turned towards Zara, staring at him from the opposite stall. "She never does. Hence she was left inside last night rather than going out with the other horses."

"Just tie her up and I'll work around her."

TJ shook his head. "I can't let you do that."

"I've done it before. Loads of times."

"I don't care. You're not doing it here. It breaks every health and safety regulation in the book and then some." He tried to put on the halter once more. "Come on."

Celeste shook her head, pawing at the ground with her left leg.

Zara pushed the wheelbarrow into the next stall. "Okay, I'll carry on over here."

Alicia plunked down a fresh wheelbarrow and picked up the full one. "She's also a fast worker. That's her sixth stable in an hour."

"A bionic worker, huh?" TJ was impressed.

"Nah. I'm having fun being around horses again." Zara wiped her brow on her sleeve. "If you don't want us cleaning around her, let me try calming her."

TJ shrugged. "Have a go at her. But you put your hat on properly, first."

"Of course." She fastened her hard hat and walked to the stall door. "Hey, Celeste. Mind if I come in?"

The horse glared at her and whinnied.

"And good morning to you, too." Zara took three calm steps towards TJ and Celeste and reached out a hand. She gently patted Celeste's nose. "That is one very pretty blaze you have there, girl. Anyone ever told you that?"

The horse eyed her with suspicion.

"Bet they don't say it enough. Now, I have to clean up in here, make it all nice and sweet smelling for you to come back in."

TJ took a step back, watching in amazement as Zara calmed the wild animal and got the head collar on her.

"Atta girl. See, it's not so bad." Zara glanced over at TJ, keeping the hand contact with Celeste. "You want her outside with the others?"

"Yes, please."

Zara clicked her tongue and led the horse outside.

Alicia whistled. "You got a genuine horse whisperer there, boss. She's a keeper."

"Yeah." He nodded in agreement. *Or she would be if I didn't have to sell.* He followed Zara outside. "How did you get so good with the horses?"

"Previous career." Her answer was still cagy. "Dad owns several. I used to work in the stables there. Spent every waking hour with them. Last three years, I never really had the chance. I'm hoping to quit my current job soon, and live in a stable."

He chuckled. "Live in a stable?"

"Yeah…no. I want to work with horses again."

"You can't beat it." He angled his head at Celeste. "She seems to like you."

Zara patted Celeste's nose as she slipped off the head collar. "Under that moody exterior is a beautiful, sweet-natured animal longing to get out and run."

"I wish I knew why she's so bad-tempered. My guess is she was mistreated by her previous owner. Or spoilt."

He glanced over at the gates as they opened. A car pulled into the yard. "Okay, time for me to go do some work. Come into the office in a couple of hours and I'll find you a uniform shirt and jacket. I'd order you some in, but it's probably not worth it for only a couple of weeks."

"You sure you don't want to hire me full time? I can call and quit my job right now this minute."

His heart sank. He'd like nothing more than for Zara to be around all the time. To get to know her better. Spend time with her, both in and out of work. He'd never felt an instant attraction before. Sparks literally flew every time he was around her, even if he was the only one who noticed the fireworks. His heart pounded. Something blocked his throat, preventing him from breathing, and he had to work to force the words out. "Uh…"

She tilted her head at him. "Is that such a bad idea?"

He cleared his throat. "I have to sell, remember?"

"Shame." Zara locked the fence. "Because Aunt Agatha said I could live with her 'til I found somewhere of my own down here."

TJ caught his breath. "You're staying?"

"For a while."

Celeste whinnied and kicked the fence.

"Hey, enough!" TJ yelled. "I know you don't want to be out here. I don't want you out here either. But I am not cleaning around you. It's not safe."

"I'll go muck out her stall, so she can go back inside." Zara paused and moved closer to the fence.

"There's something wrong with her."

"I don't have time for her now. I have a session in the school room. It's probably her temperament."

She shook her head. "No, it's more than that. Let me lunge her."

"We've never managed that. She won't let us." He sighed. "I'm honestly thinking the best thing would be putting her down. Only I can't afford the vet's bill."

Shock covered Zara's face. "You can't do that 'cos she's moody. You'd have to shoot me once a month in that case. Let me try."

"Okay, Miss Horse Whisperer. But you be very careful. I don't want you getting hurt."

Zara glanced sideways at him. "Why not?"

"Because I'd have to call an ambulance and fill in a shedload of paperwork." He pulled a face, not about to divulge the real reason. "The lunge lines are hanging in the tack room with the head collars. Best of British."

Ringing echoed from the other side of the yard. He groaned.

"What's that? Do you have a phone out here?"

"Only my mobile. It's in the muck heap somewhere. It can stay there."

"What if the call is important?"

"They can ring the landline." TJ rubbed the back of his neck.

Two kids ran across the yard. "TJ!"

"Morning, boys." He shook off the anxiety the ringing phone caused in the pit of his stomach. "Today, I thought we might clean some tack, and then ride around the indoor school. How does that sound?"

Dylan and Simon cheered.

TJ laughed. "Is that for cleaning or riding?"

"Both," Dylan yelled. "Mum never lets us clean anything. She says we'll break stuff, then there'll be he—heck to pay."

TJ frowned, even though the kid had adjusted his language just in time. "What did I tell you about swearing?"

"Don't do it." Dylan scuffed his shoes in the gravel.

"Exactly. Anyway, not being allowed to clean is kind of weird. My mum insisted on my cleaning my room all the time. Then if I was really good, I was allowed to dust the lounge or her room. Which was great, 'cos it meant I could move all the ornaments. And have a good nose through my dad's cufflink boxes."

Zara chuckled. "Remind me to try that one at home. Dad would be thrilled."

TJ winked at her. "Sure. Try that one at home." He turned to the boys. "Right. The tack room awaits. Zara, you might want to grab that lunge line before we start cleaning. Else you might never get through the door."

From where he cleaned with the boys, TJ could see Zara working with Celeste. That woman certainly was a horse whisperer. He'd never got anywhere with the animal, but Zara had calmed her and now somehow persuaded her to lunge. Albeit slowly and with difficulty, as Celeste kept slowing, stopping and definitely favoured her front right leg.

Once his session with the boys was over and the tack was sparkling, TJ headed back to the office. The answerphone flashed, which he'd expected as the muck heap had done nothing but ring almost solidly for over an hour. TJ dropped into his chair and hit the button, settling back to listen.

"You have fifteen new messages. Message one. *TJ, it's Xavier. I need to speak to you urgently. Call me.* Message two. *TJ, it's me again. Call me.* Message three. *TJ...*"

This time TJ grinned. Xavier sounded seriously naffed off. Good. His American pen pal had a far more succinct way of putting that phrase, but it contained the f word and was not something TJ would even think, never mind say.

"*What is the point of having a phone if you don't answer it? Ring me.* Message four. *Mr. Greggson, this is Melanie Smythe at Abernethy Bank. I was hoping to speak to you in person, but I can't get hold of you on any of the numbers you gave us. I'm afraid we're unable to help you with a loan or mortgage at this time. I will write and confirm this.* Message five. *TJ, ring me.*"

Messages six to eight were more refusals from banks and loan companies. The remaining nine through fifteen were from Xavier.

Hands curled into fists as the anger and frustration building all morning finally got the better of TJ. He yelled as he lashed out, sending the answerphone crashing to the floor. "That's it then. I've lost everything." His eyes stung and he strode to the window. Gazing out at the only home he'd ever known, a strangled sob escaped his constricted chest. His heart clenched and ached, his stomach twisting into a cold, hard knot.

There was no point even fighting this.

He'd been born here, something Xavier hadn't been. Although according to his mother, his own birth hadn't been planned that way. His father and grandmother delivered him, whilst on the phone to the emergency services, during the worst October storm in five hundred years. He'd taken his first steps in the large family room. He'd learnt to ride on Old Chestnut. He'd helped the vet deliver Tog and decided to keep her for his own. Tog, not the vet.

He managed a faint grin at the image. Okay, now he'd passed into hysteria.

Zara stuck her head around the door. "The muck heap is ringing again."

"Let it," he muttered. He shoved his hands into the pockets of his jodhpurs, desperately trying to bottle his emotions before she picked up on them.

"What do you want me to do now?"

"Beds, haylage, ignore the ringing muck heap. The field needs poo picking before we turn the horses out for the night." He kept rigid; the slightest movement would be his undoing.

"Sounds good." There was a pause. "Are you okay?

You sound…off."

"Fine."

"Liar. But okay, you're fine."

TJ growled and spun on the spot. "Don't you talk to me like that! I can sack you in a heartbeat."

Zara held her ground. "Actually, you can't. I'm volunteering. Besides, you need me, remember?"

He glowered, not trusting himself to reply. The phone pealed. He ignored it.

"And I'm needed outside." She tossed her hair and backtracked to the door.

The answerphone spoke from the floor. "*TJ, it's Xavier. Your brother. I know you're there. Answer the flaming phone, will you?*"

"No, I will not answer the bloody phone!" TJ yelled. "I am tired of you pestering me." He broke off. "Now see what you made me do? I never swear. In fact, I don't allow the kids to do that. Told the boys off earlier for it."

Zara raised an eyebrow. "There's a poem about that."

"About what?" He stared at her.

"Swearing. Mind you, the word bloody is in the Bible. Look it up if you don't believe me. The King James version."

"Oh I will." He sucked in a deep breath. "This poem. What is it?"

Zara stopped in the doorway. "I lost a tiny little word, just the other day. It was a naughty little word I didn't mean to say. But then it wasn't really lost when from my lips it flew. Because my brother picked it up and now he says it, too."

"I probably did get it from him, to be honest." TJ drew in a deep calming breath. Not that it worked. "I'll clear up in here, and then be out to help."

As Zara left, he gathered all the papers from the floor and shoved them higgledy-piggledy into the top drawer. He slammed the answerphone back onto the desk and willed it to spontaneously combust. *I suppose I should retrieve my mobile. Then it can go in a drawer, too.*

Stomping outside, he grabbed the spade from where it rested against the wall. Six long strides took him to the muck heap where he started searching for his phone. Dig it out with his hands or grab the spade?

"Need help?" Zara's cheerful voice broke through the dark clouds surrounding him. A pair of long gloves dangled in front of his nose. The type they used for delivering foals.

He held out his hands. "It's a bit late for me."

She pulled on a pair. "Not for me." She pulled out her mobile and glanced at him. "What's your number?" TJ told her and she typed it in rapidly. Next she rang him and put her foot where the ringing sound came from. Then she started rooting through the muck heap. "Why'd you throw it on here, if you don't mind me asking?"

"Because it's a pile of poo."

She grinned. "Very funny, but I meant your phone, not the actual muck."

"Like I said. It's a pile of poo."

She dug for a minute, and then grinned in triumph. "Is this it?" She held the handset aloft.

"Zara, I love you. I could kiss you."

She scrunched her nose. "I'd rather you didn't, 'cos you're kind of pooey yourself right now. As is your mobile."

He grabbed the offensive item, glowering as it rang yet again. He wiped the screen on his jodhpurs, answered the call and hit speaker. "Xavier, hello. What do you want?"

"You actually answered." Amazement tinged his brother's voice. "Did you even get my messages? All seventeen of them."

"I did. By the way, just so you know, you're on speaker right now, and there is a lady present, so please be very careful what you say."

"Why am I on speaker?"

TJ grinned at Zara. "Because my mobile is covered in muck and I am not putting it anywhere near my face."

"What? You're not making any sense. Anyway, the reason I'm calling—"

"I'm sorry. I can't chat now, as I have too much to do. There's loads of yard work to be done. Then I have to start checking job adverts; find somewhere to live, that kind of thing."

"Why?"

"Because some idiot is determined to sell my inheritance, leaving me homeless, jobless and—why am I even bothering? You're not listening. You never do. All that matters is you and what you want. Forget anyone else."

TJ hung up and held the offending item over the muck heap once more. "Do I?"

"After all the effort I put in to find it?" Zara slanted her head and shoved her glasses up her nose. "Well, you do have to clean it. How waterproof is it?"

TJ chuckled. "I like the way you think. Let's find out." He turned on the yard tap and filled a bucket. He dropped his phone from a height, loving the huge plop and splash as it sunk below the surface.

He turned on the tap again, washing his hands and arms underneath the cold rushing stream of water. "You are a bad influence, woman."

"So I've been told." She threw the gloves away and tugged down her shirt before it rode up any further.

"However, I do owe you one for finding the phone in the first place." He scrubbed it clean of muck and held it up, water pouring from the handset. "Oops."

"Dump it in a bag of rice and put it in the airing cupboard for twenty-four hours."

"I won't ask how you know that. How can I repay you?"

"That's a bit extreme." Zara emptied the bucket.

"I'm serious. I owe you. I would offer you a job, but…" He shrugged.

"Okay, then. How about dinner?"

"Sure. Tonight?"

Zara shook her head. "Aunt Agatha is expecting me. She always cooks too much, so why don't you join us?"

"I wasn't angling for an invitation…" Although if she insisted, he wasn't going to refuse. He didn't cook for himself, instead living off microwaved ready meals. He didn't remember the last time he'd had a proper home-cooked dinner.

"She'll be fine with it." Zara waved her hand and yanked her clean phone from her jodhpurs. "Aunt Agatha, hi, it's me. Yeah, having fun. I was wondering if dinner would stretch to one more tonight." She winked at TJ. "Great, thank you. We'll see you later. Should be home around six, six-thirty." She hung up. "See. Dinner soon as we get there."

"Thank you. I'll be ready as soon as you're done here at six. I can give you a lift."

She nodded. "That's very kind, but I won't be able to get back in the morning if you do that. I hired a motorbike, so I'll go home on that."

TJ baulked. "A bike?"

She stuck her hands on her hips. "What? Don't women ride them?"

"It's not that."

"I'm not going to crash," she said. "I already promised Aunt Agatha that. I also promised I'd trade it in for a car. I'll buy one if I'm staying here."

He studied her. He hoped she would and his heart raced at the thought. Then twisted, as he realized that she might be staying, but he'd be leaving for who knows where.

CHAPTER 4

IN THE END, TJ GAVE Zara a fifteen minute head start to allow her time to change before he arrived at Agatha's. On the front seat beside him were the two bunches of flowers he'd bought at the garage on the drive here. Like most petrol stations, this one had the mini supermarket attached. He parked close to the curb and tried to calm the hornet's nest in his stomach as he walked up the front path. He rang the bell, hoping Zara didn't answer as his nerve might very well fail him. And this wasn't even a date. Even if he had bought flowers.

Agatha answered the door, a huge smile spreading over her face. "TJ, how lovely. Zara didn't tell me it was you that she'd invited."

"I can go away…" He began to turn, not sure if he was welcome or not.

She grabbed his arm. "Don't be silly. Come on in. Zara will be right down."

TJ stepped over the threshold and held out one bouquet. "These are for you."

"Thank you. They're beautiful."

TJ placed the remaining bunch on the stairs, whilst he slid out of his coat and shoes. He really didn't want to get any dirt on the cream hall carpet. The jacket he hung on the coat stand, shoes lined up neatly beneath. He picked up the flowers and followed Agatha to the kitchen.

"I must say," she said, filling a vase with water, "this is quick work even for Zara."

"Oh, no, this isn't a date. I asked her to dinner tonight. She said you were cooking and asked me here."

"But it isn't a date?"

"No, it's a thank you."

"O-Kay…" Agatha shook her head. "Why?"

"He tossed his phone in the muck heap yesterday so he didn't have to answer it." Zara spoke from the doorway.

TJ spun around. His jaw dropped before he gathered the presence of mind to close his mouth. She was stunning. Her hair was tied up in some fancy way, her jodhpurs replaced by a floral, figure-hugging dress that brushed the tops of her knees. *Wow…*

She grinned at him. "I retrieved said mobile from said muck heap and he was so grateful, he chucked it in a bucket of water."

"In my defence, you told me to do that. Besides, I

wasn't going to wave it anywhere near my face in that condition." He turned to Agatha. "It's currently drying in a bag of rice in the airing cupboard. Also Zara's suggestion. Inviting her to dinner was a thank you for saving the phone."

"As are these." He held out the flowers to Zara. "For you."

Her face broke into a huge smile. "Oh, thank you." She reached up and kissed his cheek. "They're beautiful. No one has ever bought me flowers before."

He coughed, cheeks burning. "Then it's about time they did." He resolved to buy her flowers again.

"Who are you avoiding speaking to?" Agatha asked, handing Zara a vase.

"Xavier. He left over fifteen messages today. All saying call me. And that was the landline. There are probably over a hundred on the mobile, if the constant ringing was anything to go by."

"And did you call?"

He shook his head. "Nope. And I don't intend to as it'll only turn into another fight. He wants to sell. I don't. I can't raise the money I need to buy him out. I don't have that much lying around and I can't borrow it. Heaven knows how much I've tried."

"How much do you need?" Zara asked.

He watched the way she arranged the flowers in the vase. "Quarter of a million." He noted the way she froze and glanced up. "Yup, quarter of a million. And that's only his share. It's twelve acres of prime real estate, plus buildings and livestock."

Agatha shot Zara a pointed gaze. Zara scrunched her nose up in reply. TJ wasn't sure what caused the exchange, and he sure wasn't going to ask. Never get in-between two women who had fallen out was his motto.

Instead, he cleared his throat. "We got left the land and everything on it when my father died. We make enough to keep going, but can't splurge. Xavier wants to start a new life up in Scotland on a croft and needs his inheritance to do so."

Agatha handed him a pile of plates. "Set the table, please."

TJ took them to the table. "He doesn't seem to get the fact that I'll lose everything. Either that or he doesn't care."

"I'm sure that isn't true." Agatha sent Zara another of those mysterious glances. "Why not sell his share and have a new partner."

TJ shook his head. "No! No way. I live in that house. It's my home—the only home I've ever known. I can't share it with someone I don't know. 'Sides the new owner might want it for himself." He slumped into a chair and rubbed a hand across the back of his neck. "Sorry, didn't mean to start ranting."

Zara dropped a comforting hand on his shoulder. "It's fine. Rant away."

"Xavier always was selfish, but this? This takes the biscuit. The entire packet of them."

"Chocolate ones of course."

He peered up at her. "Huh?"

"Chocolate biscuits are the only ones worth eating.

Or stealing." She put a dish of veg on the table.

"Oh, right. I'm with you now." He managed a faint smile. "It just…" He broke off unable to find a word that fitted in polite conversation.

"Sucks is the phrase Jordan would say." Zara sat beside him. "And then get told off for saying it."

"You are only allowed to say sucks in relation to a straw." Agatha set a dish of stew on a mat. She plonked onto the chair opposite them. "Yet another innocent English word the Americans have another meaning for."

TJ snorted despite himself. "Tell me about it. I used 'blow me' in a phone conversation with my US pen pal the other week only to have him hang up on me in disgust. Took me a week to get ahold of him and find out what I'd said wrong."

Zara raised an eyebrow. "Do I want to know what that means in American English?"

TJ shook his head. "No, you don't."

"Poor innocent phrase meaning to knock me over with a feather in proper English," Zara grinned.

Agatha shook her head. "I'm surprised you two get any work done. TJ, will you say grace before this gets cold, please."

TJ winked at Zara. "Grace before this gets cold, please." Then before Agatha could respond, he grabbed her hand and Zara's and prayed. On reflection that was a bad idea. He had no idea afterwards what he'd said, or whether he'd blessed the food or the inhabitants of Outer Mongolia. His mind was crammed full of the way Zara's hand felt in his. His heart pounded so loud his ears ached. His throat swelled and obstructed his breathing. His chest constricted making him light-headed.

He was a complete and utter mess.

Somehow, he opened his eyes.

Agatha grinned at him. "Thank you."

His gaze bounced from her to Zara, who also tried not to laugh, her cheeks an attractive shade of rose. "What did I say?"

Zara chuckled. "It was lovely. Let's eat, shall we?" She picked up the dish of veg, serving herself. Her phone rang. She ignored it, handing the dish to TJ.

Agatha glanced at the screen. "It's Jordan. You'd better answer. I will break my cardinal rule on this one occasion."

Zara sighed and grabbed the handset. "Usually, I like your no-phones-at-the-table rule." She slid the phone screen to the left and stood. "Hey, bug. What's up?"

TJ began to pile food onto his plate, trying not to eavesdrop as Zara left the room.

"How's she getting on at the stables?" Agatha asked.

"We call her the horse whisperer." TJ inhaled the mouth-watering scent of stew and jacket potatoes, his stomach gurgling in anticipation. "It's incredible the way she deals with them. She can calm even the most bad-tempered of animals. I'm sure she's got more experience than she's letting on."

"She has. Did she tell you she's moving in here for a while?"

He nodded. "And that she's quitting her job. I'd hire her in a heartbeat, but the way things are right now,

62

there's no point."

Zara's voice rose in the other room, but not enough to make out the words, just the emotion.

"Someone's not happy."

Agatha nodded. "She's probably talking to her father. To say their relationship is volatile is an understatement. She needs to get as far away from him as possible. Which is why I've asked her to move in here for the time being."

TJ loaded his fork carefully. "Can I ask…when I said grace, what exactly did I say?"

Agatha chuckled. "You thanked God for the lovely Zara I had made and asked Him to bless her to our bodies."

Horror filled him and his face burned. He was sure he was now bright red. "I didn't…"

"You certainly did."

Mortified he wasn't sure how to respond. "I am so sorry…"

"It's fine." She waved her fork. "Don't worry about it. Zara will have forgotten about it by now."

The door flung open. Zara flounced into the room, slinging her phone onto the worktop. "I would chuck it, but there are no muck heaps within throwing distance." She dropped into her chair, and folded her arms around her middle. "He's taken Jordan's phone away. I could hear Dad yelling at him, telling him off for daring to contact me. Then I get it in the neck for giving him a phone."

Agatha didn't appear at all sympathetic. "He *is* way

too young for a phone, you know that."

"I'm not stupid. It's a plain phone that rings and does nothing else. The only number he has is mine as how else is he meant to get ahold of me? Dad won't let him talk to me at all now. Jordan says he's being a bully. I'm the only one who really cares for him, loves him, and now I'm stuck here miles away…"

She broke off with what sounded like a sob, and buried her face in her hands.

TJ could see her fighting for control and wanted to comfort her somehow, but didn't know how or what to say. Instead he took another mouthful of dinner. He assumed Jordan was Zara's younger brother that her father didn't have time for. He wasn't about to ask for details of what was obviously a private family matter.

"Like I told you last night," Agatha said, "we'll figure something out. Now eat."

Zara huffed and stabbed her fork into her meal. She shovelled in several mouthfuls. Finally she looked up. "He makes me so mad. I don't want Jordan being pushed like I was. Not with school or study or whatever career he decides to go into eventually."

"He won't be. He isn't old enough for school yet, anyway." Agatha studied her niece across the table. "Do you regret your career choices?"

"No. Only the way it ended." Zara sighed. "Maybe Kim is right."

"She is not. Your sister is very much like your father, and has the ability to only see things from one viewpoint. They are right and everything else is—"

"Folly," Zara finished.

TJ put his fork down and picked up his glass of water. "Sounds like we both have enough family problems to sink a battleship."

"Certainly do." Zara glanced at him. "Let's change the subject. I hope you don't mind or think I'm interfering. Alicia said you had problems reading— hence the specially made chart in the office."

"Alicia has a big mouth." TJ plonked his glass down firmly, with a scowl. His cheeks heated once more. "My dyslexia isn't something I want advertised or like talking about. It doesn't make me slow or stupid or an idiot or any other definition you can think of. And I can read. Kind of."

"Please, just listen, okay?"

He jerked his head. "Two minutes."

"It was the way you described the words jumping on the page." Zara twisted in her seat to face him. "I used to know someone who has the same trouble. It's called colour dyslexia."

His attention caught, he turned to face her fully. "What's that?"

"You've seen the celebrities with their coloured glasses, right? Blue, yellow and so on."

"I thought that was a fashion thing."

She shook her head, pushing her own glasses back up her nose. "Nope, it isn't. The different lenses refract the light properly so they can read like everyone else."

Sceptical, he studied her. "Really?"

"Yes. There's an optician here in town that knows all

about it. Found that online as well. It has to be worth checking out."

"Blue and yellow, huh?" TJ pondered the idea. He knew of an actor and a musician who wore glasses like that.

"Different people need a different colour spectrum. You might need red or green or a combination. What do you think?"

"I'll sleep on it."

"Stubborn man." Zara rolled her eyes. "If you're anything like my father, that means no. Ring them now. I'll even dial it for you. You can leave a message, and have them call you back in the morning."

"Nothing to lose, right?"

"And everything to gain." She grabbed her phone and dialled.

TJ took the phone from her and waited to leave a message. He almost jumped when a real person answered. "Oh, hello. I didn't expect anyone to still be there."

"It's late night closing," the female receptionist replied. "How can I help you?"

"I'd like to see someone about…" TJ faltered, forgetting what it was called.

"Colour dyslexia," Zara said helpfully.

TJ shot her a thumbs-up. "…colour dyslexia," he finished.

"Certainly. We have an appointment at ten-thirty tomorrow morning. Can I have your name please?"

"TJ Greggson."

"We'll see you in the morning."

"Thank you." TJ hung up. "Tomorrow at half ten."

Zara grinned. "And you don't even have to ask the boss for time off during work hours."

He handed her phone back. "You knew they'd still be there, didn't you? Railroading me into this."

"Yup." She grinned. "Payback for that lovely grace you gave earlier."

He shook his head at her. "You wait. Poo picking duty for the rest of the week."

She sniggered. "I'll simply change the colour scheme. Then you won't know which is which."

Agatha laughed. "Okay, enough children. Go and sit in the other room while I do the dishes."

TJ shook his head. "You should go and relax. That was a wonderful meal. My first proper home-cooked dinner in months. We'll wash up."

Agatha held up her hands. "I'm not going to argue." She rose and headed to the door. "Coffee would be good too."

Zara grinned. "Nothing changes. I'll put the kettle on."

TJ dumped a load of dishes in the sink. "And I'll wash up."

"Fine by me." Zara stood and cleared the rest of the table. "I don't like washing up, anyway."

"Seriously?"

She nodded. "Yup. I hate it."

He turned on the hot water. "Strange woman. I hate drying."

"There you go then. We're a perfect match."

TJ added the washing up liquid, watching the bubbles form and multiply in the water. Was her comment an offhand one, or did she mean something more by it? Either way, there was no harm in asking, right?

He sucked in a deep breath. "So, I was wondering. Did you want to go and see a film tomorrow night? I'm not sure what's on. We could just pitch up after work and choose one that sounds good."

"Are you asking me out?"

He kept his eyes on the sink, not wanting the water to overflow and flood the place. "Kind of. Not out, out, if you didn't want that. More one friend showing another one a good time…" His cheeks burned. "No, that's not right. We are friends, right and you don't know anyone else here and…"

"Relax, TJ. I'd love to go to the cinema with you tomorrow night. Thank you."

He glanced at her. "We leave the phones at home. I don't want my brother ruining things." *Or your little brother, Jordan, either come to that…*

"Sounds good to me." She grabbed the tea towel. "Ready when you are."

Zara sat next to TJ in the garden in her aunt's picnic chairs which had seen better days. She sighed contentedly. "I do so love the summer evenings. Look at it—almost nine-thirty and still daylight, never mind warm enough to sit outside." She hadn't bothered to put a cardigan over her sleeveless dress and wasn't remotely cold.

TJ sipped his coffee and stretched his legs out in front of him. "I went to visit my pen pal in Nevada several years ago. Even at the height of summer it was dark by eight. We sat around a fire pit on the campsite toasting marshmallows."

"Ohhhh." She set her cup down on the wall and jumped to her feet. "I will be right back. She ran inside, grabbing the few things she needed, before running back to TJ. "Okay, we have matches, sticks, and marshmallows."

She dropped them into his lap. Then she placed the incinerator on the patio. Making sure it was level, she set it up and removed the lid. It took her less than a minute to get a fire started. She sat down and grinned. "There."

TJ set his cup down. He ripped open the package of marshmallows.

Zara opened the packet of wooden kebab skewers and handed him one. She took a marshmallow and speared it. "Take that." She held it over the fire.

TJ followed suit. "I hope you're not expecting me to sing."

"Of course."

He laughed. "Because I don't. I only sing, very badly, in church."

"Don't worry about it. Psalm 100 says make a joyful noise, not a tuneful one. I usually end up singing kids songs these days."

"Do you sing to Jordan?" he asked. He turned his stick over. "How old is he?"

"Three." She ate her mallow. "Mmmm. I should do this more often."

"Good aren't they?"

"Yeah." She stabbed another one. "So my singing these days consists of worms with daft names, men in flying saucers, travelling on a bus, and hats with three corners. Other than that, a few action songs from church."

"My favourite one is the 'Wise Man Built His House upon a Rock.' "

She nodded. "Jordan loves that one. Especially when the house goes splat at the end. He also likes 'Ten, Nine, Eight'; 'Who's the King of the Jungle'; 'Jesus is the King' and 'My God is so Big'. Although Jordan is convinced it's *my God is so big and as strong as my nightie…*"

TJ roared with laughter. "We sing a couple of those. I don't know the jungle one. How does that go?"

Zara broke into song and after a couple of times through, TJ joined in. She tried not to pull a face. He wasn't kidding about being unable to sing. She grinned as he impaled three mallows at once. "Is it quiet there without Xavier?"

"I thought I'd miss him more, but… No, in some ways I do."

"His paperwork skills?"

"Not only that. He was always there. If we had a

problem, we'd solve it together. Only now he's gone and taking everything with him."

"Have you asked why?" She ate her mallow slowly and licked the sticky stuff off her fingers.

"It turns into a fight and I end up hanging up on him. He wants a new start and thinks crofting is it. Only it won't be. He used to be full time at the yard, with the horses. Then he decided he wanted to work in an office, so took over the books. Then he wanted to be a mechanic. Then a barista. Then a waiter in a restaurant. Then a chef. He kept doing the books for me, but he was hardly ever here."

"Now he wants to be a farmer."

"Yup. That's why I don't want to sell. It'll be a five-minute wonder again. But he's gone and put the yard on the market and made an offer to buy the freehold of the croft. It's gone too far to stop now."

Zara shook her head. "As a fifty per-cent land owner, he can't sell without your permission. You can block any sale by refusing to allow it." She shouldn't be telling him this, but she wasn't going to let her father destroy this man if she could help it. Or his brother.

"I can?" Hope glimmered in his eyes.

"Yes. I've seen it loads of times in my line of work. Call the estate agent. Tell him the yard is in joint ownership."

"Xavier won't like it."

Nor will Dad. "That's too bad. You need to do it before someone puts an offer in and your brother accepts it. Tell the estate agent that you both have to agree to the sale and sign any paperwork. You also need to get your lawyer involved and up to speed. As well as the solicitor who oversaw the reading of the will, just in case there is anything in that which would prevent the sale. And you need to do it fast."

"I'll see to it first thing in the morning. Remind me."

She chuckled. "I would send you a text, but there are three problems with that. Your phone is practically dead as you keep trying to kill it. You don't answer your phone when it rings. And finally, you couldn't read any text I sent anyway. At least not until after you've been to the opticians."

He waved his stick at her. "Oy, pick on the dumb bloke why don't you?"

She stole his marshmallow and popped it into her mouth.

"That was mine," he complained.

"Want it back?" She opened her mouth and stuck out her tongue.

TJ held up a hand. "No, thank you for the offer, but no."

Raindrops began to fall, not a gentle rain either, but a sudden downpour that had them running for the house.

Zara shut the kitchen door and flicked on the light. "Wow. Is that the time? It's almost ten-forty-five. And dark."

"I hadn't noticed. I've been enjoying myself." TJ pushed his hands through his wet hair.

Zara stifled a yawn. "Me, too."

"I shall let you get to bed. Can't have you falling

asleep at work in the morning and blaming the boss. People will talk."

"Let them."

TJ shook his head. "Too much of a gentleman for that. I'll see you at work."

She saw him to the front door. "Good night. Don't forget to call the lawyer and estate agent first thing."

"I will. Night."

Zara closed the door and turned, almost colliding with her aunt. Her aunt frowned at her. Zara widened her eyes and tried to appear innocent. "What?"

"You just can't help yourself, can you?"

She stuck her hands on her hips, defence mode taking over. "Actually, I was telling him his rights. Told him to insist both he and Xavier have to sign everything as they are co-owners and told him his brother can't sell without his permission. TJ is different. I like him."

"You hardly know him."

"I know enough. Besides, I'm not about to jump into anything. I have Jordan to consider."

"You know TJ probably thinks Jordan is your kid brother, right?"

"Oh." Zara stopped short. "That explains a couple of things."

"You have to tell him the truth. Before things get any more complicated."

"TJ is my boss." Zara wrapped her arms around her middle. She wished he wasn't only the boss, that there was more between them. A lot more. But it wasn't likely to happen. No matter how much she would like wishes to be horses so that beggars may ride.

"Uh-huh." Aunt Agatha didn't let up. "I've seen that look in your eyes before when you talk about someone special."

"Daniel," she whispered. The ache in her heart returned, although much diminished from the searing pain it used to be.

"Yes. Daniel."

"It isn't the same thing. Daniel was…" She broke off. Tears pricked her eyes. "You know very well who he was and what he means to both me and Jordan."

"It won't ever be the same with someone else. But you can't lock yourself away in some ivory tower and hide your feelings. You have to live again. For Jordan, if not for yourself. TJ is a good man. Don't play with his feelings. That isn't fair on him. And if you do, you will have me to deal with. Understand?"

Zara rubbed her neck. "I don't intend to mess him about. I told you, I'm tired of the way Dad does business. That's why I'm quitting."

"Have you done that yet?"

She shook her head. "No, purely because Dad still has Jordan. Otherwise I would."

Aunt Agatha held her gaze. "Once Jordan is here?"

"I'll quit working for Dad." Zara paused. "TJ asked me out tomorrow night."

"Are you going to go?"

"I said I would." Rain pounded against the windows. "I hope it's not like this in the morning," Zara said. "The bike will be no fun if it is."

"I'll drive you in," her aunt said. "You should buy a car as you're staying. Ask TJ to help you pick one out."

She shook her head as she headed up the stairs. "You don't give in, do you?"

"Course not. I'm a Michaels. We never give in."

Zara sighed. Maybe it was time she didn't give in either. Fight for what she wanted. Her son and…

The word *TJ* whispered in her heart.

CHAPTER 5

IN ALL HIS TWENTY-NINE years, TJ had never known a storm to rival this one. Rain poured down from a blacker than normal night sky. Although, on reflection, *poured* didn't even begin to cover what this storm did. He had to pull over several times on the drive home as he was unable to see where he was going—even with the wipers going full blast.

He parked as close to the house as he could, still getting drenched running from the car to the front door. The key jammed in the lock and it took a minute for his wet fingers to make it work. Once inside the house, he grabbed the hand towel from the downstairs bathroom and dried his face and hair.

The horses weren't happy. Even with the door shut he could hear them whinnying. He assumed they were huddled under the single tree at the far end of the field. Should he bring them in? Normally, as it was summer, he'd leave them out all night. But this was no normal rainstorm.

The pounding rain continued unabated. Opening the front door, he gazed out. His mother used to say it was coming down in stair rods, his father would say cats and dogs or Japanese car parts.

Decision made, he pulled on his yard boots, full length waterproof coat and the bright yellow sou'wester that Xavier always teased him about. He headed first to the tack room. Unlocking the door, he flicked on the light. This place was a mess. Whoever was meant to tidy it last hadn't done a very good job. He pulled all the head collars off the respective pegs. At least he knew which one belonged to which horse without reading the labels Alicia attached for the rest of the staff.

The downpour blinded him as he splashed across the yard to the stable block. He unlocked the door, sliding the key on the hook inside the door. Celeste kicked her door. TJ turned on the light. "I don't blame you in the slightest. I'm going to bring in all the others. Won't be long."

He turned sharply, and plunged back out into the deluge. Splashing his way across the yard, he headed to the field. The horses stood under the tree on the far side. Mud squelched under his boots. Sheets of rain hurt his head as it hit his sou'wester. "Hey, guys."

TJ got collars on four of them. "Come on. Let's go." He took two in each hand. "I'll come back for the rest of you."

The horses came with him. Tog followed of her own accord. They pranced and sidestepped, jerking heads, whinnying.

"Yeah, I don't like it either." He made it back to the stables, seeing the horses into their stalls. He pulled off the head collars and bolted the doors behind each horse. Water dripped off them to the floor. The thin summer rugs each horse wore clung to them like a second skin. "Let me get the others inside, and then I'll deal with the rugs. I'm on my own here."

TJ ran back into the driving rain. The water was now over the toes of his boots. At this rate, he'd be wading back to the house. The remaining four horses went with him willingly, not wanting to be out in the storm any longer.

Once all the horses were safe inside, TJ set to work stripping off wet rugs, rubbing down and putting dry rugs on each animal. He could leave them un-rugged, but wasn't going to risk any of them getting sick.

Celeste whinnied and kicked her door. "Hey, ease off." TJ glanced across the stable at her. "I am not feeding anyone. It's the middle of the night."

Finally done, he headed to the doors and flicked off the light. "Good night. See you in the morning." He locked and barred the stable door and waded across to the house. The yard was completely flooded.

"And that, dear brother, is why I insisted on spending all that money building the stables a foot above the yard. I'll even send you a photo in the morning. Assuming my phone has dried out." TJ climbed the steps to the house, grateful to be out of the pelting rain. He toed off his boots and hung his wet things in the hallway to dry. He flicked off all the lights, bar the single bulb on the landing. Taking the stairs two at a time, he headed straight for his room.

He glanced at the clock as he turned on the bedside lamp. Gone two in the morning. Hardly worth going to bed, but he would. He tugged the curtains closed, only to whip them open as the rain turned to hail, hitting the tilt-and-turn windows with enough force to break them, had they not been double-glazed. The sound was deafening with the window open the couple of inches at the top. He hated sleeping with the window shut.

Glass shattered outside. "There goes the green house. More mess to clear up in the morning."

Lightning split the sky in two, illuminating the whole yard for a few seconds. TJ jumped. They hadn't forecast a storm. He counted to ten before thunder echoed. The hail increased in volume. Thunder crashed again. The horses whinnied and stamped, but at least they were inside. TJ shut the bedroom window.

His grandmother would open them all during a thunderstorm, along with the front and back doors, but he'd rather stay shut inside. Safe and dry—without all the mopping up of wet floors Granny had to do after the storm finished. Of course, Granny would also cover all the mirrors and hide the silverware every time it thundered.

He headed into the next room, overlooking the yard

and field. Thunder boomed again, closer this time. Multiple flashes of lighting seared the sky. TJ watched awestruck, humming 'How Great Thou Art', the words resounding in his mind.

A huge flash split the heavens. Thunder immediately echoed as the tree in the end field burst into flames. "Whoa!" TJ stepped back from the window. His heart pounded, stomach clenched. That was close.

He'd been standing right there, with the horses, not that long ago.

Torrential rain kept the fire in check, flames crackling, as he watched in horror. At least lightning didn't strike twice in the same—

There was another bright flash. Almost as bright as daylight, with a hint of blue. Electricity sizzled. All the power went out.

The house rocked beneath his feet.

An explosion propelled TJ across the room, slamming him into the wall. He landed on the floor in a crumpled heap, dazed, his ears ringing.

The hairs on his arms and head stood on end. He opened his mouth, working his jaw in an effort to relieve the pressure. He shook his head, trying to calm his breathing down.

His nose twitched. Something was burning, but the smell wasn't smoke. It seemed to be more electrical.

What had the storm hit now? Must've been close whatever it was.

His whole body hurt as he rolled over and pushed himself upright. Staggering in the dark, he made it to the door. He flung it open and was about to step through when something held him back.

Find a torch.

Not one to ignore the voice in his head or common sense, TJ backtracked and, using his hands to feel along the wall, found the torch from where it sat on the bookcase. He inched back to the door and shone the light into the hallway.

Only there was no hallway.

The part of the house where his bedroom was, where he was about to step, where he should have been sleeping, was gone.

CHAPTER 6

ZARA ARRIVED ON THE MOTORBIKE shortly after eight. Two fire engines blocked the parking bays, so she wheeled the bike around the back of the stable block.

Where was TJ? What had happened overnight? She left the bike and ran into the yard. "TJ! TJ, where are you?"

"Here." TJ stood in the yard, boots on, sweeping water towards the drains. It must have flooded in the storm last night. Obviously the fire department was here to help with the clear up.

She moved over to him. "Are you okay? Did the place get flooded?"

TJ turned to face her, leaning on the broom. He looked awful. Bags under his eyes, scrapes on his hands and was that blood on his face?

"What happened?" She moved closer.

"We got struck by lightning. Twice. It took out the tree and the house."

The house? Shock resonated. "Are you okay? Were you in the house?"

"Yeah. I'd just got the horses in. They were sheltering under the tree, but the rain was so bad, I couldn't leave them there." He pointed to the burnt remains of the tree in the field. "Right now, we have nine pretty spooked horses. I haven't fed them or anything yet."

"We'll get to them. Your ear is bleeding."

TJ reached up and touched his ear, but his fingers came away clean. "Not anymore."

A fire-fighter came over. "We've done what we can to make the place safe. The roof is gone, but other than the central span, the ground floor is pretty much undamaged. I'll send a crew back over this afternoon to check there are no more hot spots. In the meantime, if anything happens, give us a shout."

"I will. Thank you."

The fire-fighter nodded. "You'll need to get your insurance assessor out this morning."

"Sure thing." TJ stood still as the fire engines drove away. He closed his eyes, letting out a deep breath.

"How bad is it?" Zara shifted her feet, itching to know if the horses were okay. "Was it only the house?"

"Come see." He set the broom against the wall, and headed around the side of the stables.

She followed him. As they rounded the building, she

stood still, unable to take in the sight of the damaged house. A neat hole had been carved right through the middle of the building.

TJ pointed. "See that door on the right, upstairs?"

She nodded. "Yeah."

"I was in the room behind it, watching the storm over the yard. I saw the tree get hit. I remember thinking that it was good I'd got the horses in else they'd have been killed. Then there was a massive flash, an explosion…" He shrugged.

"Wow. Good job you were in your room."

"I wasn't."

"Oh?"

TJ pointed to the hole. "See that missing chunk of house? *That* is my room. Or it was." The horses began to whinny in the stable blocks. He sighed.

She reached out and grabbed his arm. She had to make sure for herself that he really was all right. "It's okay. I'll go see to them. Do you want them in the field once they've been fed?"

"No. I need to check it's safe first. And deal with the remains of that tree. It will need chopping down."

The other staff began to arrive.

Zara glanced across the yard. "We'll deal with that. You go get some coffee and something to eat."

"Not hungry," he muttered.

"Stubborn man."

Alicia came running over. "Are you okay?"

"I'm fine." TJ's tone was short and abrupt. "I need the top field gone over piece by piece to make sure it's safe for the horses. The remains of the tree need felling. The yard is still flooded. The horses need feeding. Jobs need doing. We have sessions due in at ten, and I am not going to put them off."

"And we can do that." Zara rolled her eyes. She pulled out her phone and sent Aunt Agatha a text. "Okay, that's Aunt Agatha mobilized to come over and help out."

"I'll go put the kettle on in the office, and organize the troops," Alicia said. "We'll have the field safe before the horses are ready to go out." She headed across the yard.

Zara turned to TJ. "See. So you can go find some breakfast."

"Which part of 'not hungry' didn't you understand?" TJ's hands curled into fists. "I have too much to do and—"

"Did you sleep?" She followed him as he marched to where he'd left the yard broom and began sweeping again. Was he a robot? Or were his insides not in knots like hers were?

"What do you think?" he asked. "And why phone your aunt? I can manage, you know."

"I'm sure you can, but she can organize stuff brilliantly. I figured she could act as your secretary today—make your calls, take notes and so on. Deal with the visitors, file your paperwork. Leaving you to do the other stuff, like horses, opticians, etcetera."

He waved a finger at her. "Don't you etcetera me."

"Then stop acting like you're a lone ship in a storm."

Zara kicked her boots through the water, watching the ripples spiral outwards. He could be such a stubborn oaf at times. "Because there are ten of us here today. All hands to the pump—literally. We can clear up and run this place as it should be. We are all here for you, like it or not."

She drew in a deep breath. "You also need to call the estate agent, your lawyer and your brother. And don't forget the opticians at half ten."

"Don't have time. I have a disabled riding session at ten."

"I can do it. It's just Daisy, yeah?" She snatched the broom from him. "So leave this to us and take ten minutes to yourself."

He snarled and furrowed his brow. "I'm not incapable, you know. I can do this."

"I never said you couldn't. I simply said you don't have to do this on your own." Zara eyed him. "Do all the horses get the same feed?"

"No."

"Then show me."

"Fine." He stomped across to the stables and unlocked the door to the feed store. He threw food into the named buckets and stacked them in two piles. "You keep them in order so it's less backtracking in the stalls. Take that pile."

Zara picked them up and carried them into the stables. "Morning, horses," she called. "Breakfast time." She made her way along the left-hand row, dropping the buckets over the doors.

Celeste eyed her and the bucket in her hand.

Zara glanced over at her. "Hey, you okay? You're not even attempting to put that leg down today. Is it really hurting you?" She dropped the bucket over the door.

Celeste ignored it, backing away on three legs.

Thumping came from behind her. Zara turned. TJ slammed his fist into the wall. Three long strides took her over to him. She grasped his arm. "Talk to me."

"Why?" TJ shook himself free.

"Something is bothering you. Or did you mean why did the house get hit? Because I have no idea as to the answer to that one."

"No! Why did God spare me? I should be dead. I should've been sleeping in that room. If I'd left your place earlier, I would have slept through the rain and the storm. Xavier jokes I could sleep through an earthquake."

"So why were you still awake?"

"Because by the time I got back from your place the rain was horrendous. I decided to bring the horses inside. That took an hour to stable, remove the wet rugs, dry and re-rug them. Maybe longer."

"Then I guess God isn't finished with you yet, TJ."

He snorted. "How'd you figure that one out?"

"You're still here. Now, coffee. And don't argue with me either." She guided him to the office. "Sit."

"I'm not a dog." TJ slumped into the chair. "But, okay, you win. This time. I'll sit for a few minutes."

Zara filled the kettle and flicked the switch. "Where are the insurance documents?"

"No idea. Xavier dealt with all that."

"Okay. And what's his number?"

"It's in my phone." TJ stared at her. "Which is in the non-existent airing cupboard, somewhere in the wreckage of the house."

Zara tried not to laugh. "Your phone got blown up. The storm succeeded where you failed."

"Yeah."

She snorted, turning it into a cough to hide it. "Well, I guess it's officially dead then."

TJ laughed bitterly. "I guess so. And I didn't do it either. Saves me the trouble."

Zara made the coffee and slid it across the desk to him.

"Thanks. His number is in the rolodex."

"Old fashioned." She opened the card file and flipped to X.

"Yeah, well." He sipped the coffee and leaned back in the chair.

Zara dialled quickly and listened to the ringtone. She wandered across to the window, staring at the house. He'd been more than lucky. Nothing short of a miracle had saved him from certain death.

She dragged her attention back to the phone.

"Hello, TJ. Little early for you, isn't it?"

"Actually, this isn't TJ. My name is Zara Michaels. I'm calling from Hebron. I need the insurance policies. TJ isn't sure where they're kept."

"Why?"

"There was an incident last night. The house was

struck by lightning and partially destroyed. TJ is fine. Little shaken up and bruised, but otherwise unhurt. Understandably he's—"

"What?" Xavier's voice changed from annoyed to concerned. "Put him on the phone now."

Zara held the phone out, but TJ shook his head. "I'm afraid he's a little busy dealing with things right at the moment. But I can assure you he's unharmed. I'll get him to call you later, but if you could give me that information, please?"

"Filing cabinet in the office. Third drawer down. You say the house was hit? Is it going to affect the market value of the place?"

Unable to believe the audacity of the man, Zara shook her head. "There is a huge hole in the middle of the house where TJ's bedroom used to be. He could've been killed. He would have been if he were sleeping. But because he's running this place singlehandedly, he was out with the horses until the early hours and still up at the time of the lightning strike. He'll live. Shame the same can't be said of the house or his mobile phone!" She ended the call and slammed the phone onto its base with a growl.

TJ stared at her, admiration in his face. "Atta girl. That told him"

"And if he calls back, let Aunt Agatha handle him." Zara paused. "And here she is."

TJ hit the button to open the gate.

Zara turned her attention to the filing cabinet. The insurance documents were right where Xavier said they'd be.

Aunt Agatha breezed into the office. "Well, that's a mess out there."

TJ glanced up. "Oh, yeah."

She put a bag on the desk in front of TJ. "I stopped at the drive-through on the way here. Breakfast. Eat it."

"Like I told Zara twice already, I'm not hungry."

"It's breakfast and it's hot. Eat."

Zara moved behind him and put a light hand on his shoulder. "It's not worth arguing. She's got that dog-with-a-bone look in her eyes." She grabbed the cordless office phone again and dialled. "Hi, my name is Zara Michaels. I'm calling in relation to a policy we have with you."

TJ tuned Zara out. He wasn't going to admit it, but the food did smell good. He swallowed. "Thing is, I feel incredibly sick."

"Kill or cure then," Agatha said decisively. "It'll either make you throw up or stop you feeling sick. Either way, problem solved."

"Fine." He opened the bag and pulled out the box as Zara headed outside, still talking on the phone. Removing the plastic lid, he inhaled deeply. The smell of bacon, egg and sausage turned his stomach, but he wasn't about to admit defeat. Agatha had a point. He hadn't eaten since last night and had been up all night to boot.

His mind strayed to Zara as he picked up the bacon. "Is she seeing anyone?"

Agatha swivelled, a mug of coffee in her hand. "Zara? No. There was someone special a few years ago, but not anymore."

"I'm meant to be taking her out tonight."

"She said."

The shaking in his hands slowed as the food started to fill his stomach. "I'm not sure I can now."

"Of course you can. Why ever not?"

He pointed out the window. "That's why not."

Zara came back inside. "Okay. The insurance company will send an assessor out this morning. They said next week, but I told them it was an emergency. They are also sending a building inspector to make sure the house is safe. Now what else can I do?"

"I don't know," he said with his mouth full.

"Manners," Agatha chided. "Let me handle the phones and so on. It beats sitting at home all day. I can also do all your office paperwork."

"You'll need to call the estate agent and TJ's lawyer," Zara said.

TJ nodded. "Yes. According to Zara, as I own half the land and outbuildings, I have to co-sign all the papers and agree to any sale. Xavier can't do it alone."

"I can do that." Agatha winked. "I used to be a legal secretary. Nothing will get past me."

"He also has the opticians at ten thirty, so he needs to leave here by ten."

"I'm sitting right here you know," TJ protested. He shoved the rest of his meal past his lips and brushed his hands on his trousers. At least he didn't feel sick anymore.

"Shut up," Zara said. She studied the board.

"Excuse me?" He rose and crossed over to her in five strides. "Last time I checked I was the boss around here."

She glanced sideways at him, a light dancing in her eyes and a faint smile on her lips. "You heard me. Shut up."

He turned her to face him. As he touched her all his nerve endings came alive. "You are one bossy cow, did you know that?"

"And it's something I'm really good at. Although did you know that a bossy cow is really a calf that's kept in a stall all the time rather than in a field? I'd prefer bossy so-and-so, if you really must insult me." She raised an eyebrow and pursed her lips.

TJ could resist no longer. He dipped his head and caught her lips with his, kissing her lightly. He pulled back and when she didn't move, kissed her again. Her hand slid up to his neck and he deepened the kiss.

Someone cleared their throat. Oh no! Agatha. He'd forgotten they weren't alone.

Zara's cheeks were a delicate shade of rose, matching the burn he felt in his own face.

"I shall leave the two of you alone for a bit." Agatha's tone vibrated with amusement.

"No…" Zara managed.

TJ cleared his throat. "We're done for now."

"I'm going anyway." The door shut behind the older woman.

Zara leaned closer. "What was that for?" she whispered.

"Being a bossy so-and-so," he whispered back. He tweaked her nose. "Thank you."

"What for?"

"Caring enough to nag."

"Anytime." She slanted her head. "Do you have a downstairs bathroom in that house?"

"Probably not one that's safe to use. Why?"

"You need to clean up a bit. You still have blood right here." Her fingers gently touched his ear. "Did you even see a doctor?"

"No. They sent an ambulance out, but I refused to go to the hospital. I was needed here. The paramedics checked me over before they left."

Agatha came back into the office. "Alicia got the showers in the stable block running hot. And I found a clean uniform that should fit you. Can't do anything about underwear…"

TJ pulled a face and put his hands over his ears. "Underwear? My house has been destroyed and you're moaning 'cos I don't have clean boxers? I can get some in town when I go to the opticians."

Zara giggled. "This is where I get being bossy from."

Agatha shook her head. "Cheeky beggar."

Zara blew her a kiss. "Love you. Right. I am going to get those horses out. They need it today. I want to check

Celeste's leg again though. I don't like her not using it."

TJ stood up. "If the field is clear, not otherwise. Leave Celeste for now. We'll take her into the indoor school later and you can lunge her again. Make sure the water trough is full."

"Alicia checked the water. It's fine." She frowned. "And I am not lunging Celeste. I'll walk her around the school sure, but she barely managed lunging last time. Go shower."

"Okay. I'm going. Those numbers are in the rolodex, Agatha. Tell them Xavier can't sell without my say-so."

Agatha nodded. "I know what to say. You're not handling this alone anymore."

"Thanks." TJ headed outside and shut the office door. He leaned against it. Had he really kissed Zara? And not a peck on the cheek either. A full-blown, full-on, knock your socks off kiss that left him wanting more. He wiped his mouth on the back of his hand. And this was with him covered in soot and who knows what else.

Agatha's voice came through the door. "Zara, you need to call your father and tell him to back off. Now is not the time for him to be pressuring anyone."

"I—"

"No. For once put someone other than yourself first."

"I am! I will call him after I have seen the horses. You call the lawyer and get a halt put on any sale they've cooked up between them."

Footsteps came to the door and TJ dodged into a side room quickly. Why would Zara's father be pressuring anyone? And what would it have to do with him and the stables? Or maybe he was reading too much into this? His tired mind couldn't make head or tail of anything.

Once Zara had gone outside, TJ headed over to the stables. A hot shower and change of clothes sounded wonderful. Well, not too hot. Just in case he fell asleep somewhere. Like while driving into town. That was a sure-fire way to ensure he didn't get the answers he so desperately needed.

CHAPTER 7

TJ ARRIVED BACK AT THE YARD. Huffing, he yanked the keys from the ignition at the sight of the farrier's white van parked where the fire engine had been earlier. "Now what?" He jumped out of the car and slammed the door. He stormed into the office. "What's going on?"

Agatha glanced up. "They're in the stable with Celeste."

TJ scowled and stomped over to the stable block. He sucked in a deep breath and sent up a telegram prayer. He'd better make the effort to be polite. Even if it was the last thing he felt like doing. "Morning, Fraser."

The farrier glanced up. "Hello, TJ. Sorry about the house. I hear you had a lucky escape."

"You could say that." TJ fixed his stare on Zara. She

stood in the stall, holding Celeste's head collar, while the farrier worked on the horse's foot. "Well?"

"I called him." Her hand stroked Celeste's nose, but she did raise her head while she spoke.

"You did, did you?"

"Celeste wouldn't even put her foot on the ground this morning. I had to do something."

The farrier glanced up. "And it's a good job she did. I assume this is your rescue horse, TJ?"

He nodded. "She's been lame since we got her. I've never met such a bad-tempered animal."

"I'm not surprised she was lame or unhappy." The farrier picked something up from the floor and held it out. "This was in her foot."

TJ took it. "A nail?"

"The kind we use to attach the horseshoe. Her shoe hadn't been put on properly. The nail missed the hoof and went into the soft part of her foot instead. The pain must have been intolerable. But she'll be fine now. Zara is brilliant with her. Held her head and convinced Celeste to let me work. She's been given antibiotics and pain killers. She'll need them a few more days as the wound is infected."

Why didn't I see that? Have I really been so distracted I've been insensitive to the animals I claim to love so much? Embarrassed and annoyed with himself, TJ jerked his head. "Thank you."

The farrier packed away his tools. "I only did the one shoe for now. She'll need it replaced again, but with the rest of them in a month."

Celeste whinnied and put her foot down experimentally.

Zara patted her nose. "I know girl, but it's better now. It won't hurt for much longer."

"I'll see you out." TJ was determined not to show his ire until he and Zara were alone.

"It's fine." Fraser shot him a smile. "I know you're busy. I'll see myself out."

TJ waited until they were alone, then spun around and fixed a steely glare on Zara. "I can't afford farrier fees to fix a horse who—"

"Hey, she can hear you." Zara cut him off. "How would you like a nail in your foot and be forced to walk on it? There's plenty of life in the old girl yet." She rubbed Celeste's nose as the horse nudged her. "See, she's loads better already."

"You're right. I'm sorry." TJ reached over the stable door and patted the horse's neck, nodding as Celeste tossed her head and glared at him. He deserved that glare as well. "I'm sorry girl. I should have called him out."

"Yes, you should have," Zara told him. "Way before now. Actually, Xavier should have had her checked over before he bought her or when he first realised she was lame."

"Aye, well the jury's out on that one. We were both at fault. He was too busy leaving and I've been too busy being angry with him to do anything other than be mad at her." He stroked her nose again. "However, it doesn't alter the fact that there is a protocol here which I ignored. That'll be two hundred quid right there in farrier's fees, never mind the call out charge and treatment. Two hundred quid I don't have, may I add."

"I'll pay it." Zara tossed her head and shot him a glare. Almost the exact same way Celeste had.

"Don't be stupid."

"Don't call me that! I called him out, I'll pay the bill." She stomped out of the stall, closing the door behind her. "How did the opticians go?"

"Changing the subject, I see." TJ sighed, but went with it. He was in it deep enough as it was without making things any worse. "You were right about that, too. I have that colour distortion thingy you mentioned."

"And they can fix it?"

"Aye. I have these rather fetching violet reading glasses coming in the next few days."

"That's great."

"If you say so. Jury is also out on that. But on the plus side, I only need them for reading."

Agatha strode into the stable, all business. "TJ, Mr. Mitchell from the insurance company is here to see you. As is Mr. Murphy, the building surveyor."

TJ's gut twisted. What if his home wasn't worth saving? And where would he live in the meantime if they deemed it unsafe? "Thanks. I'll be right there." He pushed a hand over the top of his head. "Guess I'm wandering in the wilderness right now after all."

Zara frowned. "Huh?"

"Jeremiah chapter twenty-nine. The bit before verse eleven. Seventy years wandering in the wilderness. Look it up. Better go face the lions, and you need to go do some work." He brushed his hands on his jeans and headed out.

Zara followed him.

Alicia came across the yard. "TJ, there you are. Kirsty is here for her lesson."

TJ stifled his irritation. "I have a meeting with the insurance blokes, maybe you—"

"No can do, boss. I'm about to lunge Rumple, then Pogle."

"I'll do it," Zara said.

TJ nodded to the other side of the yard. "Kirsty has special needs. Her mother is very particular about who does what with her."

"And?" Zara planted her hands on her hips. "She's a kid who wants to ride a horse. I know what I'm doing."

TJ raised his hands, too tired to argue further. "Fine. Have at it. Just don't blame me when her mum lays into you." He leaned against the wall, staying within shouting distance in case he needed to wade in.

Zara headed quickly to the young girl in a wheelchair and hunkered down next to her. "You must be Kirsty. I'm Zara."

"Where's TJ? He usually does Kirsty's lessons." Mrs Jones wasn't happy if the scowl was anything to go by.

Zara glanced up. "He has to deal with storm damage today. The stables got struck by lightning last night." She turned back to Kirsty. "So, I offered to take you out instead. Which horse do you normally ride?"

"Forgive me for being rude," Mrs Jones began. "But who are you? I haven't seen you here before."

Zara didn't take her eyes off Kirsty. "Zara Michaels. I used to ride horses for the British team. Who do you normally ride, Kirsty?"

"Sparkle. I have a special saddle."

Zara nodded. "I've seen it, and it looks really cool. Shall we go and tack Sparkle up? Would you like to use the outdoor school or the indoor one?"

"She usually uses—"

Zara stood up. "I asked Kirsty. Why don't you go across to the parents' lounge and make some coffee, Mrs Jones? We'll come and find you after Kirsty's lesson."

"I…"

Zara began to push the wheelchair over to the yard, leaving Mrs Jones stock still, open-mouthed.

TJ grinned from where he still leaned against the wall. "Nice one, Zara," he whispered pushing upright properly. Wishing she would handle the next meeting for him as well, he headed into the office.

Agatha stood as he entered. "TJ, this is Frank Mitchell from the insurance, and Ted Murphy from the builders."

TJ shook hands. "Gentlemen, shall we?" He turned to the door. It'd be so nice if whoever kept kicking the hornet's nest in his stomach would pack it in.

"Is that Zara Michaels over there?" Ted Murphy asked.

"Aye." TJ widened his eyes in surprise. "How do you know her?"

"I know her father. Besides there isn't an equestrian fan in the country who wouldn't recognize her. Is she working here now?"

"For the moment, yes."

"Nice one. She's even prettier in the flesh than on TV."

TJ glanced over at the object of the conversation. Who was she? He'd have to search her up online. Time for that later. "Okay, the damage is to the centre of the house and mainly upstairs. The fire brigade will be back later today to check for hot spots, but they said it's safe for now. Well, safe being a relative term. I do need to get back in though. I have nowhere else to sleep."

Ted Murphy cleared his throat. "Well, I can tell you, merely by looking at it, you won't be going back in there any time soon. Not until that central part has been fixed. Not even to get anything out. It isn't safe."

TJ closed his eyes, breathing out deeply. He'd have to hire a caravan. More expense. Good job his faith was secure, otherwise he'd been in deeper trouble than he already was.

Zara stood by the fence, watching the horses. Almost time to go home. TJ had made himself scarce all day. No surprise there. She and the other employees had spent the afternoon fashioning a shelter in the field. Building regulations meant permission would be needed for a proper outbuilding, so they'd thought outside the box. And, she had to admit, she was rather pleased with their invention.

She pulled out her phone and checked it. Her father had read the message, but not replied. Not sure if that was a good thing or not, she slid the handset back into her jodhpur pocket.

TJ joined her. He pointed across the field. "What is that?"

She grinned. "What does it look like?"

He leaned his arms on the fence. "It looks like someone put a great big table in the middle of my field. And a giant one at that. Dare I ask why there's a table in my field?"

"The horses needed a shelter as there isn't a tree anymore. Buildings need planning permission. Furniture on the other hand doesn't. So we built an oversized table as a temporary solution to the problem. And before you ask, it didn't cost a thing. We used all the wood lying around the place, along with the old stable doors."

He sucked in a deep breath. "I owe you an apology."

"For?" She wasn't going to make this easy on him. He'd behaved like a class one idiot.

"For not calling the farrier myself, for not listening to you about Celeste, for the crass comments about her, for calling you stupid. I'm under so much pressure here, I'm cracking and my temper is short and…"

She smirked. "It's okay, TJ. We understand. You're a bloke and you can't help being unable to multitask. And you've had a very bad day, so we'll cut you some slack."

He shook his head. "I'll ignore that one for now. Is everything done?"

"Yes. What did the builder say?" She turned to face him, leaning her back against the fence.

"The house is repairable. Insurance will cover it. They'll rush the paperwork, but I can't live in it until it's finished." He twisted, nodding to the caravan being connected to the water and electricity. "Hence my new temporary home."

"Nice. Presumably the repairs will hold up any sale."

"I'm praying so. Ted Murphy the builder seemed impressed you were working here. Apparently he knows your father. He did say something strange though."

"What's that?"

He turned and faced her, one elbow on the top of the fence. "He said every equestrian fan knew who you were, so evidently I'm the only one who doesn't. He added something about being prettier in real life than on the telly. Now, how would he know any of that?"

Zara shifted and changed the subject really fast. "Are we still on for dinner and a movie tonight?"

"Yes." His eyes narrowed.

"My treat."

"I ask you out and you pay? How exactly does that work?"

"Well, as we have to take you clothes shopping first for an entire new wardrobe because your clothes went up in smoke, I figured you'd be broke. And I owe you for calling the farrier out." She held his gaze, praying he'd go with the distraction, at least until she'd had time to formulate a reply that wasn't going to upset him.

TJ pointed a finger at her. "That's a very good point."

"So, how about we make it shopping and dinner tonight? You can pay for the movie next time…assuming there is a next time."

"You're on. But I'm picking out my own clothes."

"I don't have a problem with that." She pushed away from the fence and began walking slowly.

TJ kept pace. "How much of everything do I get? I've never replaced everything at once before."

"Aunt Agatha suggested she makes you a list…" She broke off as he laughed. "Take me home so I can change and we'll go before she realizes we've gone."

An hour later, after the fastest clothes shop ever, TJ studied at the trolley. For a woman, Zara had excellent taste in men's apparel. She'd suggested a week's worth of boxers and socks, eight tops, two pairs of trousers and a jumper. He'd also picked up a jacket, suit, tie, and dress shirt, which cost him a small fortune.

Now he was grateful he wasn't paying for dinner as well. TJ left his shopping with Zara while he changed into the suit. He stood in front of her. "How do I look?"

She smiled. "Very smart. I feel totally underdressed."

He eyed the floral sleeveless dress she wore. "Rubbish. You look great. Slightly overdressed for the fast food joint over the road though."

Zara giggled. "I was actually going to take you to the Toby Carvery. I asked Aunt Agatha to book a table earlier."

"Crafty. What if I'd already booked somewhere?"

"Too bad. In any case, they only hold the table for ten minutes past the booked time before it's available for walk-ins."

The restaurant was busy. The waiter led them to a table in an alcove under the window. TJ pulled out a chair for Zara.

"Thank you." She sat and put her bag by her feet.

"Can I get you anything to drink?" the waiter asked.

"Grapefruit and bitter lemon," Zara said.

TJ stifled a grin as she then had to explain to the waiter exactly what that was and how to make it. He decided to keep his order simple. "I'll have apple juice, please."

Zara rolled her eyes as the waiter left. "I can't believe he didn't know how to make that. Have you ever been here before?"

TJ shook his head. "No."

"Then you're in for a treat. These restaurants are set up the same all over the country. We go and get the food from the counter—four choices of roast and as many veggies as you can fit on the plate. Dessert gets brought to the table along with coffee when we're ready for it."

"Sounds good."

A teenager at the next table rose and came over. "Excuse me, but are you Zara Michaels?"

Zara smiled and nodded. "I am."

The teen shot a knowing grin back at her own table. "I told them you were. Please may I have your autograph?"

"Of course. Did you want a photo as well?" Zara signed the piece of paper the girl held out.

The teen beamed. "That would be great. Mum said not to ask, but…" She pulled her phone from her pocket.

"It's not a problem. TJ, could you do the honours?"

TJ nodded. He took the phone and shot several photos. "There you go."

The girl smiled. "Thank you so much. Have a lovely evening."

"You too." Alone again, Zara turned to TJ. "Thank you."

TJ studied her, one question forefront in his mind. It had troubled him since the builder mentioned it earlier, and then she'd studiously avoided the subject. But now she was being asked for autographs? Who was this woman who sat opposite him? Did he know her at all? He opened his mouth to ask, as the waiter appeared with the drinks.

"Can I get you a starter?"

TJ shook his head. "Not for me? Zara?"

She shook her head. "Not if I want pudding."

The waiter smiled and retrieved the menus. "Then help yourself to the carvery when you're ready."

"Thank you." TJ let the waiter leave, and then stared at Zara. "Who are you?"

"Your stable girl."

"No, I mean who *are* you? Who is Zara Michaels that's she's been on the telly, that people ask for autographs and photos?"

She studied her hands. "You didn't do an online search?" she whispered.

"I want you to tell me."

She sucked in her bottom lip and took several deep breaths. She finally raised her eyes. "Okay. I used to ride for the British Equestrian team."

The waiter cleared the dinner plates and still TJ hadn't spoken a word. Zara had never had such an uncomfortable meal since she'd told her father about Jordan.

"Can I get you dessert?"

"The peach melba sundae, please."

The waiter turned to TJ. "What about you, sir?"

"Just coffee."

The waiter nodded and left them alone.

Zara sighed. "Are you ignoring me now? You haven't said a word all evening."

"What do you want me to say?" he hissed.

"Anything is better than nothing."

"He scowled. "Maybe you want me to ask how many medals you won? Or ask if I can have your autograph?"

"Certainly you can. And a photo." The humour fell flat, and she leaned back in her chair, determined not to let the tears blurring her vision fall. "You know, maybe this is why I didn't tell you. Because it'd change things. I don't get recognized much these days. It's been a good four years since I competed."

"You still didn't tell me."

"Oh grow up, TJ." Zara leaned forward, frustration tinting her voice. "I didn't want to appear big-headed. Or to know more than anyone else. Or to be treated differently. But yes, I rode for the Britain. I did cross-country, show jumping, dressage, all of it. And if you must know that's at Olympic, World and Commonwealth standards."

"Were you any good?" Was that a hint of admiration in his eyes? Right now, she didn't care.

"Four gold—three of them individual ones. Two silver. But that was in the past. Now I'm a stable girl, and I work for you."

"To be precise, you volunteer for me. You work for your father."

"Not anymore. I quit working for Dad by text message this afternoon." She narrowed her eyes. Irritation twisted every fibre of her being, and her quick prayers were all that held her temper at bay.

"Bet that went down well?"

She shrugged. "He's giving me the silent treatment, as well."

TJ held her gaze. "I still can't pay you."

"I'm not asking you to!"

"Why did you quit riding?"

She sucked in a deep breath, letting it out slowly. "It's complicated and not something I like talking about." Pudding arrived. Along with the coffee and she waited until they were alone before continuing. She picked up her spoon. "It wasn't exactly my choice to leave the team."

He studied her. "Can you still do the fancy dressage stuff? You know the sideways dancing?"

She nodded, grateful for the change of subject. She studied the layers of ice cream, crushed raspberries and sliced peaches. "My horse, Pipkin, is the one I rode."

"Bring him up here. Show me. Actually," he sipped the coffee, "we usually have a fayre in July. You could do an exhibition thing—show the kids how it's done."

Did she really want to do that? Somehow, what came out of her mouth was, "Okay."

He reached over and touched her hand. "I didn't mean to upset you. I…"

"It's fine. Most people clam up or get really ditzy. Your reaction was—refreshing." She licked the ice cream off the spoon. "This is delicious."

"I still owe you that hack you paid for on your first visit."

"Tomorrow. If I am staying here, I'm going to need to buy a car rather than hire that bike. Both you and Aunt Agatha hate the thing anyway. Would you come with me?"

"Of course." TJ picked up his coffee spoon. He stretched over the table, and dug the spoon into her ice cream. He raised the spoon to his lips. "There is one condition."

"What's that? Other than sharing my pudding?"

His eyes twinkled. "Well…"

She pushed the glass dish into the middle of the table.

"Consider it shared."

He grinned, licking the spoon clean. "I was thinking more of you going out with me."

"We are out."

He chuckled. "Funny. I meant properly. As in boyfriend-girlfriend going out."

Zara held his gaze. "Never dated a celebrity before then?"

TJ kept his face deadpan. "I want to cross it off my to-do list." He took another chunk of ice cream, taking his time licking the spoon. "I like you. A lot. You probably worked that out from the kiss earlier."

She tilted her head. "Well, I was kinda wondering if you kissed all your stable girls like that, especially in front of their aunts."

He held up his hands. "In my defence, I'd forgotten she was there. The fact you're famous doesn't bother me. I want to get to know you better."

"One condition. The next time you kiss me, my aunt is not in the room."

He glanced around the room, then grabbed her hand and kissed her fingers. "There."

Zara laughed. "Problem is, you may find you don't like what you discover."

"We all have secrets. You know my biggest one—the whole being unable to read properly thing."

She took another mouthful of ice cream. "Yeah."

"So will you?" He gazed at her wide-eyed, expectant, fear of being rejected almost radiating from him. "Go out with me? See where this goes?"

Zara's bag rang. She sighed, and pulled out her phone. "I have to take this. It's my father. Hold that thought, and I'll be right back." She stood and headed away from the table. "Dad, what do you want?"

"You can't quit. I forbid it."

"Hah!" She pushed the doors open and made her way into the cool, fading evening light. "Forbid? You can't."

"I need you on this project. I've spoken to Xavier Greggson. He's agreed to sell at more than the market rate. I'm still making a massive profit here. The only sticking point is his brother. I'll fax you the papers. Make sure he signs them."

"He doesn't want to sell, and I'm not going to make him. In fact, I'm doing everything I can to make sure the land isn't sold."

"You will do as you are told. Work on him. Date the bloke. Convince him to sign or you will never see Jordan again."

Her stomach twisted. "*What?* Jordan is mine! You can't stop me from seeing him."

"You are an unfit mother. You abandoned him time and again. That's neglect. The phone issue—it's hardly an age appropriate gift. See what the courts make of all this. I am going for full custody."

"You can't. You send me on all these trips and I already told you I quit. I want my son here with me at Aunt Agatha's."

"You are not seeing him until that land is signed over to me." The line went dead.

Angry tears slid down Zara's cheeks. She wiped them

away. How could he do this to her again? Why did she believe his lies, his promises? She shoved her phone into her bra and wrapped her arms tightly around her middle. A huge sob escaped before she could stop it.

Footsteps came up behind her and she moved to one side, so as not to block the path. "Sorry…"

"Hey," said an all too familiar voice. "I paid the bill, got your bag."

She turned, wiping a hand over her eyes. "I must give you the money for it."

"There's no need—are you okay?" Concern shone in his eyes, overflowing into his voice. His hand touched her arm. "You're crying. What's wrong?"

"I…" Her voice broke and huge sobs made her body shake. She was dimly aware of TJ pulling her onto one of the benches outside the restaurant and holding her tightly.

After a minute or so, she glanced up. "Sorry." She fished in her bag for a tissue.

"It's fine. You christened my new suit for me."

"Least I wasn't sick on it." She blew her nose and wiped her eyes. "Jordan did that to Dad once. He went ballistic."

"What did your father say to upset you? Assuming it was him and not another caller."

She sniffed. "He wants custody of Jordan unless I retract my resignation. He reckons he has a good case. He's accusing me of neglect, abandonment. Says I'm unfit. Yet he sends me on all these trips. It's one of the reasons I quit."

"Whoa, whoa, back up a bit." TJ tucked her hair behind her ears, turning her face to his. "I thought Jordan was your brother. Surely your father already has custody of him."

Zara blinked against the traitorous tears that began to fall again.

TJ gently wiped them away, kissing her forehead. "Zara, honey, if I'm to be your boyfriend, that means I care and there have to be no secrets. Who is Jordan?"

She breathed deep. "He's my son."

CHAPTER 8

A MILLION QUESTIONS STILL NIGGLED in TJ's mind the following morning. Zara had promised to explain when they went riding. She didn't want to be overheard by anyone and wanted time to process her father's threats. When she hadn't turned up by quarter to ten, worry began to creep into his mind. He made his way to the office to phone her, finding her lingering by the gate waiting to be let in.

He cocked his head. "Five nine five one seven. And you're late."

Zara tapped in the code and apologized as the gate swung open. "I returned the bike and got a taxi here. No one was answering the intercom, so I was toying with scaling the fence. Aunt Agatha is picking me up tonight."

"I'll take you to get a car this afternoon if you like. Right now, you need to go and see Celeste."

"Okay, let me dump my bag and—"

"No, Zara. You need to go and see Celeste immediately."

His words hit home as the bag she held fell from her hands. "Is she all right?"

He mimed zipping his mouth shut. "Just go and see her, already." He grinned as she took off running. He grabbed her bag and set off after her.

Zara ran to the stables, skidding to a halt in front of the end stall.

Celeste whinnied, pleased to see her.

"Hey girl." Zara reached out, patting the horse, her voice thick with emotion. "How are you doing?"

TJ reached her side. "She's better. Lots better. Thought you could take her for a walk on the lunge line. The farrier said light exercise for a couple of days—let her set the pace."

"Sure." Zara beamed. "So am I forgiven for calling him out?"

"I'll let you know when the bill arrives. Although honestly, I'm kicking myself for not having noticed there was something seriously wrong with her." He cracked a smile. "You've probably saved me a fortune. Right, plan for today. We're going hacking at eleven and taking lunch with us."

"Okay."

He gripped her hand. "Zara, look. I am not going to give up on us before we've even begun. We both have secrets and a past, we know that. But there is nothing so impossible we can't get over."

"What if this is?"

"Give me a chance to figure it out once you explain. And honestly? Being a single parent isn't the end of the world." He slid her bag onto her arm. "Okay, dump your stuff and lunge this one. I have a session with the boys. I also want this stall scrubbed completely. Remove every possible sign of infection. I'll get someone started on that, but you'll need to help as well."

"Yes, boss. I'll get her collar and lunge line." She winked. "Are you going to the office?"

"Yes, why?"

She handed him her bag. "Be an angel and put this away for me?" She batted her eye lids. "Pretty please with sugar and cherries on the top."

"Fine." He blew her a kiss and turned, heading back to the office. He dropped Zara's bag on the floor and turned to Alicia. "Do me a favour? Call Agatha Michaels and see if she can come in and help out again this morning? I would do it but the kids have just arrived—I have all four of them for the next hour and a bit." He hit the button to open the gate.

"Sure."

"Thanks. I'll be with the boys if you need me. Zara is lunging Celeste so if you could make a start on her stall, that would be great. It needs deep cleaning. With the meds Celeste is on, the last thing she needs is another infection." He nodded to the computer. "What are you reading?"

"I did a search on Zara. Have you seen this?"

He studied the screen. Zara stood on a podium, gold medal around her neck. "Yes, she told me. Four gold, two silver. She also said it was a long time ago and she doesn't want a fuss made. However, she has agreed to do an exhibition dressage for the summer fayre. Maybe you and the others could join in as well. Jumping and so on. Not a competition, so you don't have to worry about falling off and making an idiot of yourself."

Alicia laughed. "That'd be you, boss."

"I fell off once. Over a year ago. Are you never going to forget that?"

"You fell off right into the water jump. It was spectacular. And no…have you told Zara that yet?"

His cheeks heated. "No, I have not." He waggled a finger. "And don't even think about it. Zara is a volunteer here. She doesn't need to know that. Not everyone in the world needs to know I fell off a horse. It really wasn't that funny."

Alicia roared with laughter. "Yeah, it really was. But…Seriously? You're not paying her. She's full time, and does more work than Charity, Matt and Edward put together."

"She has…had a job. She quit yesterday. Maybe I should hire her and sack those three."

"Snap her up fast, before someone else does." She winked. "And not just jobwise either. I happen to know she's single."

"Get on with you." TJ wondered if his feelings were really that noticeable.

"I'm being serious. You like her and she likes you. It's obvious."

Okay, his feelings *were* that noticeable.

"Actually," he said. "I have it on good authority, that Zara has a boyfriend."

"Really? And when did you discover that?"

"Last night, over dinner, right after I asked her out." He winked. "Apparently, her boyfriend is me."

Alicia high-fived him. "Way to go, boss. Now just tell your brother where to go and save the stables and all our jobs."

"I wish I could." He grabbed his notebook from the desk and headed out into the sunshine.

Dylan, Simon, Marty and David stood there, mouths open as they stared at the ruins of the house.

"Did you burn your house down?" Dylan asked.

"Nope, the storm did that all by itself."

Marty's eyes rounded. "Wow. Were you in it?"

"I certainly was and it was rather scary so I don't want to talk about it."

"Mummy says you should talk about scary things so they go away."

TJ ruffled Simon's hair. "That's only the monsters under the bed. Now, I'm going to need a lot of help this morning. How good are you four at writing things down?"

"Really good," the four boys chorused.

"That's great, because we have a summer fayre to plan and I can't read my own writing."

"That's a bit of rubbish," Simon commented.

"It certainly is not." TJ pointed to the classroom. "Let's go."

"Do you need glasses to help you read like Dad does?" Dylan asked. "Did they burn in the fire as well?"

Taking the way out, TJ nodded. "I've ordered a new pair with special violet lenses to help."

"Wow."

"Yes, wow indeed. Now, get into that classroom and find the huge pads of paper. We need to get planning so this can be the best summer fayre ever."

Zara poked her head around the door and smiled. TJ bent over the table, engrossed in his work, all four kids helping him with words and pictures. "It seems like a lot of fun in here. And I'm sorry to interrupt, but TJ has a visitor in the office and it's time for maths."

The boys groaned.

TJ glanced up. "Already?"

She nodded. "It's gone eleven."

"Boys I'm sorry. We'll leave it there for now."

"Can we carry on next time?" the blond kid asked.

"We certainly can. Zara, come and look at this."

She crossed the room and grabbed the huge sheet of paper. "Wow, such a lot of ideas. Summer fayre, huh?"

"We're helping to plan it," another child said. "It's gonna be the best ever. See, we got stalls, rides, a bouncy castle, music and even a question thing."

"Equestrian," TJ corrected.

"Yeah, what he said. With a medal winning rider coming. Course the other staff will ride too. TJ might even fall into the water again. You should have seen it, it was so funny. Over the jump, over the horse's head, and into the water. Splash!"

Zara laughed as all the boys made splashing sounds and matching hand movements. "I would have loved to see that. The fayre sounds wonderful and with this much enthusiasm, it'll be the best in the county."

"Okay, enough embarrassing me." TJ's cheeks were a cute shade of rose. "Go and find Miss Val before she has my guts for garters."

The boys ran off.

"And you can forget what you heard."

Zara stepped closer. "Really? Which part? Because I'm serious. This whole thing sounds amazing."

The light vanished from TJ's eyes. "Going out with a bang," he whispered. He pushed upright and started gathering the papers. "Who is this visitor you mentioned? Only I don't recall a meeting and you and I have a lunch hack arranged."

"Aunt Agatha. She said you asked her to come in."

"Yes. I did." TJ pointed to the papers. "Can you put this someplace safe, please? How did Celeste do?"

"She did great. She's putting some weight on that leg now and seems content in the field for once."

"Good, I'm glad. Give me ten minutes with your aunt and we'll go on that ride. Tack up Rumple and Tog and I'll meet you in the yard. I'll bring the basket with me."

Zara turned to the sheaf of papers as TJ headed out. She stacked the sheets and searched for a box. There wasn't one anywhere in sight. A tall cupboard stood in the corner of the room. She pulled out five unlabelled box files. The top one was empty, so she placed all the papers in that and labelled it.

The next three were also empty, so she stacked them to take back over to the office. The bottom one was full of what appeared to be legal documents. She pulled out a couple. Neither made much sense, not even to her. Her conscience hit her hard, but she rationalized there could be something here of importance. The next one was an envelope marked *will*. She opened it up and read. Dated four years ago, it stated the land couldn't be sold for a minimum of ten years after TJ and Xavier inherited. Unless one of them bought the other out. Then they held it for their lifetime, on the proviso the land was used as a stables.

Zara glanced over at the office, then put all the documents back. She labelled the box *Hebron* and placed it back in the cupboard, piling all the other box files on top of it, labels facing inwards—the exception being the summer fayre one.

Her mind whirled. That paper would stop both his brother and her father in his tracks. It would save TJ's birth-right and give him time to obtain the money for his brother some other way.

A piece of paper she'd missed filing away fluttered to the floor. She stooped to grab it. A codicil. If either brother were to leave within the ten-year time frame, he forfeited his inheritance.

She shoved it into the box. Closing the door she leaned against it, breathing heavily. In the office TJ and her aunt appeared deep in conversation. This was what he needed. But while her father still wanted the land, still had his claws into Xavier and still kept Jordan, she didn't have a choice. She had to keep schtum.

That wasn't a sin, was it? To keep quiet a little longer. After all, it wasn't like anyone knew the papers were there. TJ would assume they'd been destroyed with the house. Or more likely didn't know about them at all, otherwise he wouldn't be in this fix. Besides, right now any sale was on hold so long as TJ didn't sign anything.

A small voice inside her whispered *sins of omission matter just as much as sins of commission.*

She shook her head. Right now, she had horses to saddle and a long, uncomfortable conversation with TJ looming. There was time for papers to be discovered later, once Jordan was safe.

Zara heaved a sigh and headed outside into the sunshine. Heat blazed down and she shoved her sleeves above her elbows. She brought Rumple and Tog from the field into the yard and tied them to the fence.

TJ met her by the tack room as she carried Rumple's saddle over to the horses. "Haven't you tacked the horses up, yet?"

"I got side-tracked. Sorry."

He held up a basket. "No idea what is in here. I was about to make us some sandwiches, but it looks like your aunt already made us a lunch."

"No, I made it. I forgot to bring it in with me."

"Even better. I've asked your aunt to work here a couple of days a week. Handle the office stuff. See if she can find any legal documents my father or grandfather might have stashed somewhere. I'm really hoping they weren't in the house."

"Papers?" Her heart pounded.

"Legal stuff. Dad's will, Grandad's will, that kind of thing. But I'm not holding out much hope. Most likely they were in the house with my mobile phone."

"We should pick you up a new one."

He shook his head. "Insurance is dealing with that. Should come tomorrow. Might need your help to set it up. If that's okay?"

She nodded, falling silent as she tacked up Rumple.

"Are you all right? You're quieter than usual."

"I'm fine." In truth, she was as far from fine as she could get. Her stomach churned and she wasn't sure how she'd manage to eat anything.

"You don't need to be nervous telling me about Jordan. I told you that." He placed the basket down and headed into the tack room to grab Tog's saddle. *Wish I knew what to do.*

"Tell you what." TJ reappeared as quickly as he'd gone. "How about we ride down the road for ten, fifteen minutes and back? Then we'll take the picnic to the park and talk. I'll drive us there and we can pick up a car for you on the way back here."

Zara stretched her feet out on the tartan blanket and tried to relax. The sun blazed down. To her left, children played on the swings and roundabouts. To the right, the paddling pool was full, sunlight shining on the ripples on the water's surface. In front of her sat the dreaded picnic basket.

TJ flopped beside her and held up the bottle of juice. "Can't believe I left this in the car."

She smiled, leaned forwards, and opened the basket, pulling out china plates and glasses.

TJ picked up one of the glasses. "Oh, I say," he said, affecting a posh accent. "Little bit upper class, isn't it? Bone china, champagne flutes…" He held up the crystal, twisting it in the sunlight. "And expensive glassware I might add."

"Aunt Agatha's picnic set. I was going to pack the food, along with paper plates and plastic cups in a carrier bag, but she insisted on the wicker basket." Zara pulled out tubs of salad, bread, cake and coleslaw. "And the *pièce de résistance…*"

TJ's eyes widened as she removed the lid. "Is that what I think it is?"

"Scotch pie."

"But you can't get them this side of the border. I've tried."

"I made it." She offered him the knife. "Want to do the honours?"

He shook his head. "You can."

Zara slid the pie onto a plate and cut it into four pieces.

TJ said grace. He loaded his plate with a bit of everything.

Zara laughed. "Only a little hungry, then?"

He angled his head and looked at her. "Umm, starved, if I'm honest. I still need to grocery shop. Kind of forgot that last night." He took a mouthful of the pie and closed his eyes, bliss written all over his face. "Mmmmmm…. Are you sure you made this?"

She grinned, biting into a small test piece of her own. If he could talk with his mouth full, so could she. "Uh-huh. Hand raised pastry and all. Though I did use lamb and not the traditional mutton. Aunt Agatha had a recipe for it. She said she got it from church."

"Mum used to make them for the church group meals. You know, the ones where everyone brings a dish? She'd make tiny ones, individual portions, for that. But we'd get to have the large ones as part of a main meal one night a week."

Zara ate slowly, combining bites of pie with the crunchy carrot and cucumber sticks. "I'm not going to ask whose is better. As its most likely your mum's recipe and most blokes would insist on mum's cooking winning hands down."

"Yours is pretty good, though. You'll have to make it again."

"With or without mint?"

"Without. The local butcher in the village sells

mutton."

"Then I shall get some and next time you can have a whole pie and not have to share."

TJ grabbed the last piece quickly. "Don't mind sharing sometimes. Except when it comes to the last bit." He grinned and shoved it all in at once. He chewed for a bit, then swallowed. "Of course, I'd want mash, swede, and green beans with it."

"For a picnic?" Zara nicked the last carrot stick before he could snatch that as well, and dipped it into the coleslaw.

TJ laughed. "No, for dinner."

She tilted her head and affected a Scottish accent. "Yer shure ye widnae rather have a haggis pie? Right along wiv tatties and neep?"

"I may be half Scottish," he said, eyes twinkling. "But I have never much cared for haggis. You know what it is, right?"

Zara pulled a face. "Are you trying to put me off my lunch?"

TJ chuckled. "Maybe. And I'd prefer swede over neep or turnip any day." He drained his glass and topped it up. "Anyway, talk to me."

"And ruin the moment?" She opened the cake and offered it to him. After he took a slice, she put a piece onto her own plate.

"Trust me, nothing could ruin this moment. Except perhaps a downpour of rain that sends us scurrying to the car. The sun is shining. I have a beautiful woman by my side. A Scotch pie that rivals my mother's in awesomeness. Now, tell me about your son."

CHAPTER 9

ZARA STARED AT THE SLICE of cake on her plate, no longer wanting it. Her whole meal lay uneasily in her stomach. So sure was she that what she was about to say would change things between them forever. After all, TJ was a Godly man. He attended church, and he'd never even gotten a speeding ticket according to yard gossip. Why would he or any other man want her now she was what her father labelled as damaged goods?

TJ laid a hand over hers. "It's okay. I'm not here to judge, just to listen."

"Jordan is three and a half."

"You have a photo?"

She pulled up the app on her phone and passed him the handset. "One or two."

TJ scrolled through them. "One or two hundred, you

mean. He's cute."

Zara gazed at the adorable blond child in the pictures—*her* child. "He makes up very unfunny jokes. He loves going to the park, playing with cars, and bricks. He'll make huge traffic jams all along the floor."

"I used to do that. Great fun."

She picked at her fingernail, not wanting to look up. "You have to understand, life was different then. I wasn't a Christian."

"I'm not condemning you, Zara. None of us are perfect. Who's his father?"

"His name was Daniel." She took the phone and scrolled up to the beginning of the camera roll. "He was a stable hand where we kept Pipkin and then he became my groom. Used to go to all the competitions with me." She blinked hard as she gazed at the photo of the two of them.

"You seem happy together."

"We were. It only happened the once."

"Once is all it takes."

Her cheeks burned. "I know. We were getting married and I guess things went too far the night before the wedding. It wasn't planned, it just…" She broke off. "Dad wasn't happy about the wedding. He said Daniel was beneath me, that I could do better than a stable boy. So we eloped. Booked a Gretna Green wedding and were driving up to Scotland. It was raining really hard. The car went off the road."

TJ gripped her hand.

Her vision blurred. "Daniel died…" Her voice

cracked and wobbled. "I survived without a scratch. I discovered I was pregnant six weeks later. I got thrown off the team—the official term is deselected. Someone told them I'd been consorting with the hired help or something, along with a dozen other lies about drug use. Dad did his best to clear my name, but it wasn't any good. Anyway, that was the end of my career."

Zara wiped her free hand over her eyes. "Dad gave me a job with his company. He hired a nanny for Jordan. I do what I can, but generally she gets there first and does everything I ought to be doing."

"You could have said no."

"No one says no to my father. He sent me away to Aunt Agatha's for the end of the pregnancy. She tried to make me stay and raise Jordan here with her, but Dad insisted I go home. He'll never give me a chance to redeem myself. He's adamant I should pay for my folly the rest of my life."

TJ glanced down at the phone again. He flicked back to the photos of Jordan. "He looks like you. No child is a mistake, Zara. They are miracles and always come in God's timing. You have a right to raise him yourself."

"That's what Aunt Agatha says. She wants me to bring Jordan here. Start a new life. We can live with her to start with, until I find a place of my own."

"Do it." He rubbed his fingers over the back of her hand. "I'll drive you up there. We'll get your son and bring him back here."

Hope flashed through her. "Y—you'd do that?"

He nodded. "Yeah. We'll take Agatha as back up.

She can distract your dad and the nanny while you and I sneak Jordan and his cars out of the house."

"You mean kidnap him?"

"You can't kidnap your own son if you're his only parent. So long as no one other than you has legal custody of him, you can take him wherever you want."

"Thank you." She released the breath she'd been holding, and heaved a deep sigh. "So, you don't hate me?"

"Why would I?" He kissed her cheek, his lips soft and warm. "Loads of kids are born out of wedlock. Fact is, Jordan's father was killed on the way to your wedding. That alone proves he was a good man. Where does Jordan get his curls from?"

"Me. I have a daily fight with the hair straighteners."

TJ chuckled. "He won't thank you for that when he's older."

"I keep hoping permed hair for men will come back into fashion."

"Oh, please. I'm hoping for a mullet. I've always wanted long hair."

She snorted, reaching out and running her fingers through his close-cropped hair. "Can't imagine you with anything other than this."

He kissed her gently, on the lips this time. "That's better. See? A problem shared really is a problem halved."

Zara hugged him, relishing the feel of the strong arms around her. "There's been no one since Daniel, and won't be until I marry."

"Like I said, we all have a past, but that's where it stays. God has dealt with it. All that matters is what we do in the here and now and in the days to come." He kissed her forehead and tucked a wayward strand of hair behind her ears.

Shivers of pleasure rocked through her, and she leaned against him. "Maybe we can come to this park with Jordan."

"Does he like football?"

"He prefers cricket."

"Cricket, really?" TJ pretended to yawn. "Never fancied that."

"Seriously? You live in an English country village, with a village green, and you don't play cricket? What kind of an Englishman are you?"

He laughed. "One who prefers playing football or watching tennis. He can teach me. Did you bring any more of that pie?"

"No."

"Then you'll have to make some more."

Zara leaned her back against his chest, nestling her head into his shoulder. "I will. Do you like the macaroni ones? You know the ones with no lid and filled with macaroni cheese?"

"Yup. And the sweet ones."

"Then I'll make both. Maybe we should have a stall of them at the summer fayre. The mini sized ones."

"Brilliant idea." He checked his watch. "We should get back and tell Agatha our plan for rescuing Jordan. We'll leave first thing in the morning."

Zara turned her head and reached up, pecking him on the cheek. "Thank you. That means a lot."

"Anything for my girlfriend." TJ winked. "We'd better make sure we pick you up a family car on the way back then."

She nodded. "And a car seat. Dad keeps Jordan's in his car and—"

"I'll call the yard and let them know we'll be another hour or so. We'll go car shopping now." He paused. "Only I can't ring, because I don't have…"

"…a phone…" Zara chorused with him, before they both dissolved into giggles. "I'll call." She pulled her phone from her pocket and dialled. "Hey, Aunt Agatha, it's me. We'll be a tad longer. We're going to get a car on the way back in. And a car seat."

"A car seat?"

"We'll tell you when we get back. TJ has a punning clan."

"You mean cunning plan."

"I was…yeah. That." Zara shook her head. The joke having fallen flat, she wasn't going to explain it.

"We'll be about an hour, tell her."

"TJ says we'll be an hour or so. See ya then." She hung up.

TJ began packing up the empty plates. "I'll drive tomorrow. Then you can sit in the back with Jordan. Have you any idea what kind of car you want?"

Zara smirked. "Yellow. And preferable a mini or a beetle."

He rolled his eyes. "Do I want to know why?"

She shook her head. "You'll find out first time you get anywhere near it with Jordan."

The following day, TJ arrived promptly at six. The drive was punctuated by music and muted conversation between him and Agatha. TJ glanced at Zara. He turned off the motorway and headed onto the main road to York. She hadn't said a word since they left four hours previously, just sat with her eyes closed. He'd assumed she was sleeping, but now she stared out of the window. "Are you okay? Not car sick or anything?"

Zara pulled out her hair band and retied her ponytail. "No. More than a little nervous. What if this doesn't work?"

"It'll work," Agatha said from the back seat. "The plan TJ and I cooked up is fool proof."

"Problem with that is Dad isn't a fool."

"Maybe he is and maybe he isn't." Agatha chuckled. "Either way, we're going to get Jordan out."

"Turn here," Zara said.

TJ pulled up to a huge iron gate. "You live in a mansion?"

"Prison, not mansion," she corrected. "The code is two four six oh one."

"Cute. If I have that stuck in my head for the rest of the day I shall blame you." TJ punched in the code. The gates opened and he drove through them.

"Follow the drive up to the house. You can park right in front of it."

TJ touched her hand briefly. "He might be out."

"And there's a flying pig."

TJ parked and the three of them got out of the car.

Zara headed up the steps and unlocked the front door with her key. Immediately a small child flew from a side room and almost knocked her over.

"Mummy!"

Zara swung him into her arms. "Hey, little bug. Mummy missed you so much. Are you okay?"

"Missed you too. Are you home forever now?"

She kissed his cheek, revelling in the warm scent of his skin. "Even better. You're coming to stay with Aunt Agatha for a bit as well. Let's go and pack."

Footsteps ran into the hall and TJ spun around.

A tall, dark haired woman in uniform blocked the stairs. "Miss Zara. Mr. Michaels left strict instructions that you were not to see Jordan."

"Jordan is my son," Zara said firmly. "And I will see him whenever and however I like."

Agatha placed a hand on Zara's arm. "You and TJ take Jordan upstairs and pack. Let me see to the nanny."

Zara nodded and sidestepped the glowering woman. TJ moved swiftly to her side and laid a protective hand on her back. Nothing was going to get in the way of him getting them outside.

Zara glanced at him. "Are you my bodyguard now?"

His chest hitched. "If I need to be."

Jordan poked him. "Who are you?"

"I'm a friend of your mummy. My name is TJ."

"What do you do?"

"I have lots of horses and run a stable."

"Mummy has a horse called Pipkin. Can he come live with Auntie Aggie as well?"

TJ grinned. "Nope, but he can come and live with me and my horses. In fact, if I can borrow your phone, Zara, I'll give them a call and get Alicia to drive up with the horse box. If she leaves now, she could be here by two at the latest. Then call your stables and tell them Pipkin is being collected and who by."

Zara set Jordan down on his bedroom floor and tugged out her phone. She dialled quickly and handed the phone to TJ. "Okay, bug. You need to help me pack all your things into these two bags. I'll put clothes in one, you put toys in the other."

TJ spoke on the phone quickly, keeping one eye on the door.

Agatha rushed in. "We have to be super quick. The nanny is calling your father."

Jordan beamed and waved his teddy in the air. "Auntie Aggie, Boxy and me are coming to your house."

"Yes, you are and it'll be fun, but right now we need to pack like the wind."

Zara flung clothes into the bag willy-nilly. "Jordan, grab only your very favourite toys and cars. I can buy you lots of new stuff later."

TJ handed her the phone. "Okay, done. She's on her way. Call your stables and get Pipkin prepped for transport."

"Why can't I take everything?" Jordan started to pout.

Agatha crossed to his side. "It's like a holiday. Just take some things."

Zara walked to the window as she spoke rapidly on the phone.

The hornet's nest in TJ's stomach kicked off again. Zara's stress and worry must be contagious. Not soon enough Agatha threw the last items into the bags and zipped them up.

Zara ended the call and slid her phone into her pocket. "Okay, done. Let's go before my father shows up. The stable will have Pipkin ready by the time Alicia arrives. I've texted her the postcode so she can use the sat nav."

TJ nodded. "Good. Gerry is prepping a stall for him. Let's get out of here."

The nanny appeared in the doorway. "Mr. Michaels is on his way home. How long will Jordan be away?"

Zara picked Jordan up and parked him on her hip, one arm holding him securely against her side. "Oh, I forgot to mention. You're fired. The only person caring for my son from now on, is me."

TJ grabbed the heaviest bag and Agatha grabbed the other. Moving as one unit, they made their way down stairs and outside to the car.

Zara put Jordan down. "Climb up here, bug. Look, you got a new car seat." She patted the seat. "I keep waiting for something to go wrong."

"Praying hard it won't." TJ threw the bags into the

boot.

"You and me both." Zara did up Jordan's straps and shut the door.

TJ nodded. He turned to Agatha as Zara got into the vehicle. "I'm dating Zara, don't know if she told you. I know Jordan will complicate things for a while, but I need to get to know her as a person, not only as a mother or work colleague."

Agatha laughed. "Is this a roundabout way of asking me to babysit?"

TJ cocked his head. "Maybe. Not every night, but sometimes."

"I will, but be warned. The first week she isn't going to want to let him out of her sight. She might even want to bring him to work."

"I don't have a problem with that." TJ slid into the car and started the engine. "So, Jordan, mummy tells me you know the jungle song and the actions."

"Yes," Jordan said, waving his arms.

"Wanna sing all the way home?" He slipped off the handbrake and started driving to the gate. His stomach wouldn't settle until he'd put at least a hundred miles between them and the danger this house posed. Singing would at least help a little. He hoped.

CHAPTER 10

THREE GLORIOUS WEEKS FLEW BY.

Zara hadn't heard from her father, except a message via her sister. According to Kim, Dad was livid over Zara removing Jordan from the house and firing the nanny. Kim had prevented him from legal action, pointing out that Jordan was Zara's son and not his.

TJ spent as much time with her and Jordan as he could. Jordan was certainly enamoured with TJ, insisting on calling him Unca Teej. It seemed a win-win situation. As for her, simply being around TJ made her heart sing, her pulse race, and the sun shine even when it was raining.

TJ dropped in most evenings for an hour or so. Either they went out or simply spent the evening playing traffic jams on the floor with Jordan and putting him to bed together.

The builders were working on the repairs to the house at the yard. Pipkin had settled well, and was great friends with Tog and Celeste, who had made a full recovery and was now the sweetest, gentlest horse anyone could wish for. Especially with children, much to Zara's delight.

Zara drove her new car into work, arriving at the yard after nine-thirty. Late, but she had a good excuse this time.

TJ opened the door of her yellow beetle. "Morning. Did Jordan get off to nursery school okay?"

"It's his first day. I'm not sure who's more of a mess—me or him. I definitely cried more than he did. That's why I'm late."

"I'm surprised you got him a place so quickly. Usually you have to wait at least six months or put their names down at birth."

"They had a space. The headmistress knows Aunt Agatha and small town, small school I guess. Plus it's only part-time. Nursery is five sessions a week, so Jordan has mornings." She grinned. "It does mean you get me and Aunt Agatha now, rather than just one of us."

He laughed. "I only need Agatha two days a week anyway, and it's no bother having Jordan here. He loves sitting in the office colouring or painting, or doing stuff with the other kids."

Zara pushed up her sleeves. "So, what needs doing?"

"Usual stuff. The horses are in the top field as the builders are too noisy for them."

Aunt Agatha opened the office door and trotted over

to them. "TJ. Phone call for you. Bloke says it's urgent. Zara, did Jordan settle okay?"

Zara watched TJ run across the yard, the hot sun reflecting off his hair. "He didn't even say goodbye. I'm mortified."

Her aunt laughed. "TJ or Jordan?"

Zara smirked. "Both. No, Jordan mainly."

"Don't be. There'll be plenty of time for the 'I don't wanna go's' to set in. He loves it here."

"I love it, too. Love being able to do all the stuff a mother should do. Even the ironing. But I love working as well. How do I balance both?"

"Easy. Buy Xavier's share of the stables."

"I wish. But I can't afford it. Not now that Dad has disinherited me."

"He can't do that."

"Well, he has. The bulk of the money is still in a trust fund that he controls. Despite the fact I am well over twenty-one, the cash only becomes mine on the day I get married. At least I opened a new bank account and transferred all my other money across before he closed those accounts." Zara gave her aunt a quick hug. "Enough complaining about stuff I can't fix. I should go and muck out. Do something constructive."

A ringing phone met TJ as he stepped into his office. Swatting the door shut, he grabbed the phone and

Zara's Folly

wandered around behind the desk. "This is TJ Greggson."

"TJ, it's Ben Steele. I have some news regarding the sale of the stables."

TJ's heart sank. He didn't like phone calls from his lawyer on a good day. And this had started out as a good day. "What sale? I halted that. Took it off the market completely."

"Xavier sold everything yesterday." Ben's tone was flat, as if he were reading the news. "He's dealing directly with the buyer."

TJ slumped into the chair as if winded and punched in the gut. Surely he hadn't heard correctly. "What?"

"The signed papers have been faxed through to me. The actual papers are with his lawyer."

"He can't do that." TJ knew he sounded like a stuck record, but he seemed stuck in that moment between waking and sleeping where nothing made any sense. "I own half this place. He needs my signature."

"It's a legally binding document. He got a court order to say he could sell the entire plot of land with just his signature."

"How?" Frustration spilled over. "This is my land, too!"

"I'm looking into that. I can contest it, but that costs money and I can't guarantee you'll win."

"I don't have that kind of money, you know that. I live here. I have the builders in right now repairing the storm damage to the house."

"That has to stop, I'm afraid. Xavier is contacting the

143

insurance company this morning. Completion is the end of the month. The twenty-eighth."

TJ glared across the room, salt burning his eyes. His gut churned and he swallowed hard, not wanting to throw up on the desk. "That fast? What about the horses and other livestock?"

"I have no idea." Ben Steele cleared his throat. "That is something you and Xavier will need to discuss. Perhaps you should come into the office. We can discuss this properly."

"Blast!" TJ's mind spun. There had to be some way to stop this. "I wish I could find Dad's will. Find out what that said. Xavier was the executor so he dealt with it."

"Like I already told you, I wasn't working here then. We can't find a copy of it anywhere. I have several paralegals going through the files in the basement. Perhaps by the time you get here, it'll have turned up."

TJ shook his head. "Knowing my luck it was in the house when it burnt down. Give me half an hour to finish up here and get into town." He hung up. Releasing a groan, he rung his brother's number. Never mind a flea, Xavier was about to get a woolly mammoth in the ear. He tapped the desk as he waited for the call to be answered.

"Hello."

"You think you're so clever!" TJ didn't bother with niceties. He let Xavier have it with both barrels.

"TJ. I was about to call you."

"Were you? When? Because according to my lawyer,

the sale of the yard has been a done deal since yesterday." Venom spilled from him.

"Yeah, about that." Xavier used his best placating tone that only ever served to annoy TJ further. "This bloke from Tennants Builders contacted me almost three weeks ago directly."

"Three weeks?" TJ didn't believe what he was hearing. "You've known about this for three weeks and you didn't bother to tell me!"

"Yeah. It's a lot of money, TJ, and I mean a lot. A full million. That's half a million each. What was I meant to do?"

"Abide by my wishes. Consult me. Not sell my only home from under my feet. You can't sell my share."

"I can, and I have. Because you would have done the same thing in my position."

TJ slammed a fist into the desk. "No! I would not." He struggled to contain the tumbling waterfall of curse words begging to be let loose. "What about the horses, the staff, the kids who rely on us? I've been thinking about Dad's will. I'm sure it said we couldn't sell."

"I don't remember that. Besides, the courts say I can. And as for your questions? Severance pay for the staff. The kids, I don't care about. Not my problem. The horses go with the land, so probably auctioned—"

"How can you say that?" TJ raised his voice further. "I don't believe this. I knew you were cold and selfish, but this goes way, way beyond that. More like bloody-minded. Don't bother calling again. Ever."

"Now who's being unreasonable?" Xavier lowered

his tone. "It's a lot of money. It's what's best for both of us. Set us up for life. You'll forgive me eventually. TJ—"

"No. Don't you TJ me. As far as I am concerned, I no longer have a brother. Because if you can stab *me* in the back like this…" Voice trembling, he broke off, beyond angry. "Good bye Xavier." He cut the call and flung the phone across the room into an old picture of him and Xavier sat by the stable block. The glass shattered with a satisfying crash.

He ripped the base station from the wall and hurled it after the phone. Then he raised his eyes heavenward. "Why?" he yelled. "What did I do to deserve this?"

At the sound of the office door slamming shut, Zara glanced up from where she carried a bucket over to the muck heap. *Now what? TJ looks livid.*

Hands clenched into fists and jaw set, TJ marched across to Zara, eyes narrowing further with each stride. "I have to go into town."

She put down the bucket. "What's up?"

"Better not say."

"TJ?"

He bit his lip. "My mother always said if you can't say it politely, don't say it at all."

What on earth could have happened? Zara grabbed his hand. "Okay, mister. Talk to me."

He gazed up at the sky and huffed. "My brother has sold this place out from underneath me."

"He can't."

"Oh, yes he can apparently. For he has." TJ stamped his foot. "Lock, stock and barrel and not just his half either. All of it."

"How?" Zara's eyes widened, shock resonating, leaving her cold and numb.

"I have no idea. But I'm going to find out." He sucked in a deep breath, which instead of calming, the extra oxygen simply fuelled the all too evident fire within him. "The thing is, I thought the will said it couldn't be sold. Mind you, I was pretty upset when it was initially read, and Xavier was the executor and would know better than me. But the lawyer didn't work there then and he doesn't have a copy—or if he does he can't find it. I have no idea where a copy would be kept if not in his office."

"Oh…"

"Are you okay? You've gone really pale. If you're still worried about Jordan and his first day at school, don't be. They will phone if he's ill."

Zara examined TJ, relieved he assumed that was the cause of her numbness. In reality she felt sick because this was probably all down to her. "Who…who's he selling to?"

"The builder who originally put in the offer. There will be over a hundred houses built here. Anyway, not that it will help, but I'm heading to the lawyers now. When Agatha gets here, can you ask her to go through

147

every single box and file, and drawer we have anywhere in an effort to find Dad's will? Although, like I said before, the blasted thing was probably in the house and long gone."

Zara shivered. She'd meant to tell him about the papers she'd found, but as time went on and the sale of the yard seemed to have been halted, the time didn't seem right or appropriate. And now...now it was probably too late, but she had to try. Perhaps she could find them while he went to the lawyers. Surprise him when he returned.

A bloke in a hard hat and reflective jacket strode over to them. "TJ, we've been told to down tools and stop work."

"Yeah, I've just been informed."

"I'm really sorry."

TJ clenched and unclenched his fists. "Me too. Thanks anyway."

The builder shook his hand and headed back the way he'd come.

TJ blinked hard, the pain in his eyes piecing her soul. "What do I do? I have to give everyone notice. Get rid of everything. I have nothing left."

"You have the caravan you're living in." Sick to her stomach, she grabbed his hand, trying to placate the furious man in front of her.

"I hired it. Thanks to my brother...ex-brother...I'm destitute."

"Don't you get half the money?"

He laughed bitterly. "Oh, yeah. Great, I'm rich, but I

have no home, no job, no family." He turned away as his voice cracked into pieces.

Zara moved in front of him, her heart breaking as she saw the unshed tears in his eyes. She raised a hand, gently cradling his face. "Yes, you do. You have me, Jordan, and Aunt Agatha. I'll talk to her. I'm sure you can stay with us."

TJ wrapped his arms around her, kissing her forehead. "I really don't think that would be a good idea, lovely though it sounds. I might not be able to contain myself."

She wrinkled her nose. "Contain?"

Red tinted his cheeks. "Control…same thing."

"Ah." She stood on tiptoes and kissed his cheek. "I love you and things will work out. If need be, you can marry me and move in properly."

TJ stood stock-still. His eyes widened. "Is that a proposal?"

She blinked. "Why yes. I think it is."

Zara didn't see TJ for the rest of the morning. He'd left for the lawyer without giving an answer to her proposal. She hadn't intended to say that, but the words spilled out and they seemed right. She wasn't about to take them back. She'd only known him a few weeks, barely time to do more than scratch the surface, but yes on reflection, she meant every single syllable.

She knew what her aunt might think—that she'd proposed to TJ in order to get hold of her inheritance. Her father would think the same thing. But that was as far from the truth as it was possible to get. She loved him. She loved being with him. Loved the way he wrinkled his nose, the way his eyelid twitched when he was stressed or upset. The fact he was great with Jordan was an added bonus.

But he had left without giving her an answer. He'd blushed deep red, stared at her, and bit his lip while that eyelid twitched. Then he'd ruffled her hair, and kissed her forehead and left.

Maybe he didn't feel the same way. Maybe it was too soon, or he didn't want a ready-made family. But she and Jordan came as a package. And thinking of Jordan had her glancing at her watch. Another half an hour and it would be time to pick him up from nursery. Hopefully he'd enjoyed his first day. But now she had a moment to spare, she needed to get into the classroom and find that box file. Assuming it was still there. It had been one crazy morning, with more work than minutes in the hour.

Aunt Agatha came across the yard. "Office. Now."

Zara leaned the yard broom against the wall. "Why?"

"Because you and I need a conversation and you don't want anyone overhearing this."

Panic made her heart skip a beat. "Is Jordan okay?"

"As far as I know. Move."

Zara followed her aunt into the office and shut the door. "Well?"

"I had a call from your father. Guess who now owns this site?"

Zara sank into the chair, catching her breath. "Who?"

"Your father. He did it because you took Jordan."

"But that isn't TJ's fault."

"You work here. TJ came with you when you picked Jordan up. In your father's eyes that makes him equally guilty. He said you were sent here to secure the deal, not put TJ off signing completely. According to him, your father simply did what you were incapable of doing."

"That's rubbish!" Zara protested. "Xavier can't sell without TJ's permission and signature. How did he do it?"

"Your father has his ways. And I searched everywhere for that will TJ says exists, but I can't find it."

Zara rubbed the back of her neck. Maybe someone else should find those papers, not her. "There's a pile of box files in the art cupboard in the classroom. I noticed them the other week. Might be worth a look."

"I'll do that." Aunt Agatha glanced at her watch. "Okay, time for you to go and collect Jordan. Bring him here. He can help me for a bit, then have that riding lesson you promised him."

"Okay." Zara headed outside, her heart in her boots. Tears pricked her eyes. This was all her fault. Maybe it was a good thing TJ hadn't accepted her proposal, because when the truth came out, he'd want nothing to do with her.

It was mid-afternoon before TJ swung into his parking spot. He switched off the engine, and gazed out over the yard. The place he'd called home since the day he was born was no longer his. It belonged to some building company. There were a hundred and forty-four houses and a corner shop planned for this land, with building permission all but granted. And all without his consent.

Zara had assured him that wasn't possible. The estate agent agreed and had taken the place off the market. Even the lawyer had agreed.

So how did Xavier get a legally binding court document allowing him to sell the whole place without TJ's permission?

He leaned forwards, bowing his head against the steering wheel. "Lord, You know how I feel about this place. It's my life, it's all I have. And Zara…she proposed. I haven't answered and probably just as well, as I have nothing to offer her. No home, no job, no security."

He caught sight of a robin hopping about on the car bonnet. "And don't mention the money. What am I meant do with it? Start over someplace else? I can't do that. I don't want another life."

He slumped out of the car, slammed the door, and then trudged across the yard, his essence splintering into a myriad tiny pieces. "This is my home. Or it was."

Dylan and Simon ran across the yard, calling his name. "TJ, come and see what we made for the fayre."

Another knot tied tight in his stomach. The fayre. What was the point in planning? There wouldn't be a fayre this year. It was scheduled for July 15th. No one would be here.

Dylan tugged at TJ's sleeve. "Don't you want to see?"

"Sure. Show me." He trudged across the yard after them. A verse from Lamentations filled his mind. *How the gold has lost its lustre, the fine gold become dull! The sacred gems are scattered at every street corner. How the precious children of Zion, once worth their weight in gold, are now considered as pots of clay, the work of a potter's hands!*

Yup, Lord, that's about it in a nut shell.

Zara met him at the door to the classroom. "Hey, how did it go?"

He shrugged. "Don't ask."

"Oh. Is it still all right if Jordan rides in a bit in the school?"

"Sure." He turned to Dylan and Simon. "Do you kids want to ride as well?"

Simon frowned. "Doesn't that cost? We don't have any money."

"It doesn't cost on Thursdays," TJ said, thinking quickly. "Zara, bring Sparkle, Ron, and Harry into the school. We'll tack them up in there. Where's Jordan?"

"In the office, helping Aunt Agatha file papers. Though I think he's being more of a hindrance than a help. I'll just grab the head collars and bring the horses over."

TJ nodded. "Dylan, run to the office and ask Agatha to bring Jordan over in ten minute."

The kid nodded and ran off. Simon started talking about the stalls for the fayre.

"It sounds great," TJ said, forcing a smile. "Can I come?"

"It's here so you have to. Can we have apple bobbing? Alicia said that's only for Halloween, but I don't see why."

"Nor do I." TJ rubbed a hand over his head. "Sure we can."

Zara led the horses over to them. "We can what?"

"Apple bobbing at the fayre," Simon said, hopping on the spot with glee.

"We should have buns on a string in that case as well." Zara winked. "And a grotto."

TJ rolled his eyes. "That's Christmas. You can't have Halloween and Christmas in a summer fayre."

"Why ever not?" Zara handed one of the horse's halters to TJ. "It doesn't have to be Santa in the grotto. It might be a fairy castle where a mystery celebrity or the old man of the woods or something is waiting for visitors."

"Does he even exist?"

"He does now." Zara looked at the boys. "Tell you what, TJ and I will have a think and see what we can do."

TJ clicked the horse into a walk and led him across to

the school. "Don't know why we're even bothering. We won't be here come July."

"Mummy!" Jordan appeared at her side, jumping like a jack-in-a-box. "Dylan said we're going riding."

"Careful, bug," Zara said gently. "You don't want to spook the horses."

"What's spook?"

"Scare them. Tell you what, you go and sit on that bench with Dylan and Simon. TJ and I will saddle the horses." She tied the horses to the fence and began to tack them up. "You sound like you've given up the fight for this place."

"No point fighting when you've lost the battle," TJ said, too quietly to be overheard. "Despite what you said about me having to agree to any sale, Xavier got a legally binding agreement to sell all of this, not just his half, all of it, with only his signature."

"How?" She adjusted the stirrups.

"This buyer made a private deal with my brother, and then got a court order or something. I have until the end of the month. June 28th to be precise. So there's no real point to planning this fayre—we won't be here. Unless we bring it forward to the 27th."

"What about the horses?"

"Xavier doesn't seem to care. He suggested I auction them. I cut him off before he could suggest anything worse than that."

Zara's eyebrows shot into her hairline. "Are you kidding me?"

"Nope. Evidently this bloke is coming for a visit

tomorrow. And to make it worse, he also has preliminary planning permission for this. No idea how. I don't remember his name, it's amongst all the papers in the car somewhere. Tennants Builders or something." TJ put the saddle on Sparkle. "One of the largest in the country. They built that new theatre in Warminster. What's it called?"

"The Adelphi…"

Why's she so pale? I would ask but probably not best to call her on it right now. Maybe she's as attached to this place as I am. "That's the one." He glanced at the boys. "Okay, lads, we're ready for you."

The kids ran over. Zara strapped helmets on all of them.

Jordan stared up at the horse, eyes like saucers. "He's big…"

"Aye, but your mum and I do this all the time." TJ swung Jordan into the saddle. "This is Sparkle. Hold the reins tightly, while I get these stirrups sorted."

"Like this Unca Teej?"

"Exactly like that."

Zara swung the other two boys onto Ron and Harry. Then she glanced at TJ. "Mind if I take little bug?"

He shook his head and grabbed the leads on the other horses. "Not at all. Okay, let's go." He headed into the school and began walking around the edge of the area. He gave the kids twenty minutes, then Val arrived to take them for maths.

They ran off with her chatting excitedly about horses and fayres.

Zara's brow furrowed. "Can you check Pipkin over? I'm a little worried about him."

"Sure. What's up?" TJ began to remove the saddles, putting them over the school wall.

"He's off his food. Hasn't been right for a day or two. I'm pretty sure it's nothing nasty, but I've quarantined him in case."

He glanced over at her. She'd been spot on previously with horses. "Yeah, I'll take a look."

"Isn't Pipkin your horse, mummy?"

"Yes, and remember, he lives here now like we do."

"Can Unca Teej come to dinner tonight?"

"If he wants to."

Jordan fixed his dark eyes on TJ. "Please. I like the way you read stories better."

Zara pretended to pout. "I thought I did the best stories."

"Unca Teej does better voices."

"Oh, I see how it is."

TJ laughed, despite the torment overwhelming him. ""I gotta worm my way in somehow."

She jumped Jordan down off Sparkle. "So it is a yes then?"

"To which question?" he asked innocently.

She held his gaze and blinked. "Whichever one you want to answer."

TJ glanced at Jordan, then back at her. "I'd love dinner tonight, thank you."

Jordan jumped up and down. "Yay. Mummy made those pies again. Only mine has macarena in it."

He tried not to laugh, imagining a dancing pie. "It does?"

"He means macaroni," Zara put in quickly.

"That's a shame. A singing and dancing pie sounds amazing. Can I have a macarena one as well?"

CHAPTER 11

TJ WIPED HIS MOUTH ON THE paper serviette and grinned over the table at Zara. "Your pies are amazing."

Zara laughed and her eyes twinkled. "You sure you don't need another one?"

He patted his stomach. "No, I think six is my limit."

"And that was the little ones. Think they'll do for the fayre?"

The joy sank to the soles of his shoes again. "There isn't going to be a fayre, remember?"

Agatha got up and began to clear the table. "Jordan, do you want to put the salt and pepper away?"

"Yup." Jordan slid off his chair and began to help.

Zara shot TJ a glance. "Don't give up. God's got this."

"I don't know." TJ wadded his serviette. "Maybe

God's trying to tell me something. Like pack up and go do something other than horses and kids and—" He groaned. "Let's face it. Half a million will buy an awful lot of straw for this little piggy to build a new house with."

Zara choked on her coffee. "How much?"

"Half a million. Each. Xavier sold for a million."

"And this bloke wants to build how many houses?"

"At least one hundred and forty-four."

She laughed mockingly. "And he gave you a million. TJ, he will make a killing on that land. Even once he's paid builders, lawyers and so on. One hundred and forty-four houses, in the country. You're talking four to five beds, garden. Even in an estate, this close to London, you're talking upwards of half a million. Each. Boy, did he see you blokes coming."

He hung his head, his dinner lying heavy in his stomach.

Zara stood. "Jordan, bath time."

"I'll take him," Agatha said.

"Want Unca Teej."

"I'll come up and read in a bit, squirt."

Zara propped her hands on her hips. "Are you giving the J-bug a new nickname?"

"Yup." TJ winked at Jordan. "If that's okay with Big Mamma here."

She threw a serviette at him. "Oy, you. Less of the big."

He grinned. "Make me."

Agatha hurried Jordan from the room. "Come on bug,

you're too young for this conversation."

TJ rounded the table and slid his arms around Zara. Just holding her, the way she neatly fit against him, made him feel so much better. "I love you, Zara Michaels." He brushed his lips against hers, and then as she sank against him, deepened the kiss. He pulled back, breathless and leaned his forehead against hers. "Do you have a middle name?"

"Athena. Kind of out there, but it's a family name. You?"

"No, but then my name is hyphenated. TJ is the short version."

"What's the long one?"

"Theo-James."

"Theo-James." Zara tucked her hair behind her ears. "I like it. And I like you. A lot."

"I should hope so after kissing me like that. And you did propose after all."

"And you still haven't replied." She grinned and tweaked his nose.

Agatha came in. "Sorry to interrupt. TJ, there's a phone call for you. It's Alicia."

"Thanks." He kissed Zara's forehead. "Hold that thought." He went into the hall and grabbed the phone. He didn't think corded phones still existed, but here was one tethered to the wall. "Hey, Alicia, what's up?"

"I was about to leave and decided to check on Pipkin one last time. He's lying down and won't get up. I know Zara was concerned all day. I think you should both come over."

TJ nodded. "Sure, we'll be right in. See you in the morning." He hung up and headed back into the kitchen. "Pipkin isn't well. Alicia is leaving in a minute or so, but thinks we should go over there. I'll drive."

The colour drained from Zara's face. "Okay. I'll get my bag. Maybe I should take my car."

He shook his head. "You're in no state to drive. I can always bring you back later."

"I'm fine to drive. I'll follow you in. Just need to say night to Jordan."

Zara dashed into the stable, her heart in her mouth. Pipkin lay on the straw. Eyes wild, he stared at her. Foam edged his mouth and a groan emitted from his chest. His stomach rumbled. She grabbed his head collar and put it on him. "You need to get up, boy. Please."

TJ came in. "How's he doing?"

"He's sweating a lot."

"Hold him still." TJ checked him over. "Pulse is raised and so is his temp. I'll call the vet, but I'm pretty sure it's colic. Get him walking."

Zara's gut twisted in fear. "What if I lose him? We lost a horse to this a couple of years ago."

"It won't come to that." TJ placed a steadying hand on her arm. "I'll call the vet. Start walking him." He raced from the stables.

Clicking her tongue, Zara encouraged Pipkin to walk

slowly up and down the path between the stalls. He kept wanting to lie down, but somehow she kept him on his feet. Frantic prayers flew heavenward. She spoke aloud, hoping her voice would calm Pipkin a little. "I can't lose this one. I'm not one for bargaining, but I will be honest if Pipkin lives. I'll tell TJ the truth and he'll hate me, but he has to know. I'll talk to him tomorrow, whatever happens."

Pipkin tried again to lie down. Zara stopped him. "You need to keep going. Please, Pip." Her beloved horse shook his head, groaning, his stomach making frightful noises.

TJ stepped over to her. "The vet is on his way. He says to keep him moving." He walked around to Pipkin's other side and grabbed the head collar. "Hey, boy, can't let you sleep yet."

"All he wants to do is lay down and roll. But if he does…" Her voice tailed off.

TJ glanced at her. "We're not going to let him."

"I don't want to go home. Not until I know he's going to be okay."

"Let's wait and see what the vet says. Best not run before we can walk."

"Okay."

They paced Pipkin silently for what seemed like an eternity, forcing him to take step after step, going up and down the length of the stable. Finally a car horn sounded. TJ ran outside to open the gate.

Pipkin stumbled and fell. Nothing Zara did could get him back to his feet again.

TJ returned moments later with the vet.

Zara's gaze flickered up, trying not to let the tears fall. "He went down. I can't move him."

TJ hugged her. "This is Kyle Matthews, our vet. Kyle, this is Zara Michaels, Pipkin's owner. They won loads of medals together. And that's famed Pipkin."

Kyle smiled and set his bag down on the stable floor. "Okay, Pipkin. Let's take a look at you."

"It's colic…" she began.

TJ moved Zara out of the way. "Let Kyle in, honey. We don't call him the miracle vet for nothing."

Zara tapped her fingers on the stall door, while the vet started work. She didn't appreciate being pushed out of the way. "He's been unsettled all day. Pawing the ground, trying to roll over and he's off his food."

Kyle glanced over at them. "TJ, can you give me a hand?"

TJ nodded. "Zara, can you go put the kettle on."

"I'm sorry?" She glared at him. "I'm going nowhere. He's my horse. I have as much right to be here as you do. More in fact."

He grasped her hand. "Give us a few, honey, that's all I ask," he whispered. "Think of it being like how a doctor asks the next of kin to leave the room when treating a patient, right? And he's feeling pretty rough, without picking up on your frame of mind."

"Okay." She reluctantly had to admit he was right. She trudged over to the office and let herself in. Eventually, she gave into the streams of tears, saturated with grief. Only when she was cried out, did she head over to the classroom to find that box file of papers, that her aunt had been unable to locate. She knew it was there. It had to be.

TJ came into the office much later with the vet. He'd half expected Zara to have come back, but she'd kept her distance. Judging by the half dozen empty cups, she'd drunk enough coffee to sink a battleship.

She rose. "How is he?"

"Sleeping," Kyle replied. "He should be fine. I passed a tube to relieve the gas. Walk him when he wakes, don't feed him until I've seen him in the morning. I've also given him fluids, antibiotics, and pain meds."

"Thank you." Relief reflected in her eyes, an almost visible weight dropping off her shoulders. "Can I get you some coffee?"

"Not for me, thank you. I have to get home. I was meant to be taking the missus for dinner, so I'm picking up takeaway instead."

"I'm sorry I ruined your evening."

He smiled. "Don't be. She should know not to organize anything when I'm on call. See you in the morning. If you need me before then, give me a shout."

"I'll see you out. But, yes honey, I'll have coffee." TJ briefly touched her shoulder, all smiles.

When TJ came back in, Zara had made two more

cups of coffee. She offered him one.

"Thank you." He sipped the hot liquid. "I needed that."

"I thought I was going to lose him."

He set the cup down and hugged her, taking in the familiar horsey smell, mixed with the floral scent that was forever Zara. "He'll be fine, I promise."

She leaned into him.

He kissed her cheek. "Maybe you should stay here tonight. The caravan has two bedrooms. I have to set the burglar alarm on the office, else I'd sleep here."

"Thanks. I'll let Aunt Agatha know." Zara pulled her phone from her pocket and sent a quick text.

TJ moved to the window, peering out at the yard. The sun was finally starting to set, despite the fact it was gone ten in the evening. He couldn't start over someplace else. He just couldn't. He feared his heart would break.

Zara's reflection in the glass drew closer. She stopped behind him and slid her arms around his waist. "Penny for them."

"Wondering what I'm going to do. Really will miss this place."

"Fight."

"No point. I've lost."

"Not yet."

He turned around and looked at her. Really looked at her. She needed to get that it was over. The battle was lost. "Yes, I have. Xavier signed it over. It's gone."

She couldn't keep the smile off her face. "Nope."

"What did I miss?"

She nodded to the table. "Nothing much. Only a big box file on the desk with something you need to see in it. I remembered a box shoved to the back of the art cupboard that had stuff in it that wasn't art related. So I went to check more closely. And guess what?"

"What?"

"I'm not gonna tell you. Go and see for yourself."

"Tell me…"

She beamed. "It's the will you needed. The one that says this place can't be sold."

"Show me." A myriad emotions slashed through him all at once. Hope flickered where despair had reigned.

Zara took his hand and led him back to the desk.

He pulled out his violet reading glasses and opened the box. *Dad's will…* He picked it up, gingerly, as if it were gold dust. "I don't believe it. Where'd you say this was?"

"Buried at the back of the art cupboard."

TJ flipped through the papers in the box, chest thumping. "This is it. This is what we need to stop the sale." He grabbed the phone. "I need to call my lawyer and tell him I need to see him first thing."

Zara watched him as he called the lawyers office and left a message on the answerphone. She hugged her stomach hard. TJ hung up. "I need to stash these in the safe. I can't afford for them to get lost again." He pulled her towards him and hugged her tightly. "Thank you. You just saved this place."

Zara hugged him stiffly.

He leaned back and studied her. "Are you okay?"

She nodded and gnawed on her lip. "Worried about Pipkin."

"He'll be fine."

"I'm going to check on him."

He kissed her cheek. "Okay. I'll put this in the safe and come find you."

Zara headed out to the stable.

TJ hefted the box file and locked it securely in the safe. He finished his coffee and washed up all the cups, leaving them to drain on the side until morning. Finally, he locked the office, and headed across the yard to find Zara.

She was on her knees by Pipkin, arms around his neck, sobbing. He moved quicker, wanting to comfort her. He stopped dead as he heard her speak.

"Oh, Pipkin. I've made such a mess of things. No matter what I do now, I lose both Dad and TJ. I should never have come here. If I'd given him those papers when I first found them three weeks ago, none of this would have happened."

TJ frowned. He took another step.

"But I've done the right thing now," she sobbed. "Surely that has to count for something. Thing is seeing his joy and relief made the grief and shame inside me ten times worse. In fact, the happier TJ gets, the worse I feel. I don't deserve a happy ending. All I do is hurt people." She wiped her sleeve over her face and laid her head on the horse's withers. "Maybe Jordan is better off with Dad."

TJ had heard enough. "No, he isn't."

Zara jumped.

TJ dropped to the straw beside her, sliding an arm around her. "You're his mum and he needs to be with you."

She sniffled. "How long have you been there?"

"Long enough. It doesn't matter how long you've known about those papers, you've given them to me now. That's what counts. Now we can stop this sale."

"'Kay."

He kissed the top of her head. "Explain one thing though, sweetheart. What's your dad got to do with any of this?"

Pipkin stirred and woke.

Bursting into tears, Zara hugged him and patting his neck.

He should drop the subject—for now. Ask her again in the morning.

CHAPTER 12

TJ WOKE AT SEVEN. He'd been too excited to sleep, like a kid on Christmas Eve, but must have dropped off some time after four AM. He dressed quickly and went into the main living area of the caravan.

The other bedroom door stood open and it didn't take long to ascertain the small building was empty, bar him. He could guess where she'd gone.

Sure enough he found Zara in the stables, leaning over Pipkin's stall door. "Morning. What are you doing?"

She shot him a smile, before returning her attention to the horse. "He's so much better this morning, see?"

TJ leaned his arms on the top of the stall wall beside hers. "Good. You, on the other hand look dreadful. How long have you been up?"

She shrugged. "Half three, four, something like that."

"Eaten anything?"

"Vet said not to eat 'til he'd been by."

TJ grinned. "He meant the horse. I mean you."

"Oh." She shook her head. "No, I haven't."

"Then you should. Come on." He grabbed her hand and led her across the yard to the office. He unlocked it and pulled her inside. "It's going to be hot again today."

Zara nodded. "Yeah. Forecast reckons twenty before ten o'clock."

He tilted his head. "Twenty—are you a centigrade woman? What's that in English?"

She smirked. "We've been metric since before you were born, mate. But, *in English,* that is sixty-eight. The Met Office reckons it might top eighty by mid-afternoon."

TJ filled the kettle and put it on to boil. "Light exercise for the horses today in that case."

The phone rang and Zara picked it up. "Hebron, Zara Michaels speaking. Yes, one moment." She held the phone out. "It's your brother."

TJ glanced at his watch as he took the phone. "Morning, Xavier. A little early for you isn't it?"

"The new owner is coming this morning," his brother said, an air of triumph in his tone. "Thought I should tell you. Oh, and be nice to him."

TJ tried to keep his voice level. "Why should I?"

"Because I said so."

TJ turned to Zara and grinned wide as he spoke into the phone. "Oh, about that. We found Dad's will last night. Along with Grandad's. I'm seeing the lawyer first thing this morning. Your court order is invalid. This sale is not happening, at least not in my lifetime."

"You can't," Xavier blustered. "I've signed."

"Co-owners. The land can't be sold. It's not happening. Ever. And from what little I glimpsed of the will, may not be allowed at all, even *if* we both wanted to sell. Which we don't."

"TJ please…I need this money."

"Don't beg. It's beneath you. I suggest you get down here fast. I'll make an appointment for Friday. You, me, the so called new owner-slash-builder, and my lawyer." He held the phone away from his ear for a moment until the obscenities trailed off. "Well, that's just too bad. Rearrange your schedule, get down here and live with it. The sale is *not happening*." He hung up, slamming the phone back on the base station with gusto.

"He's not happy I take it?"

"No, but that's tough. I won't be here as I'll be at the solicitors this morning. When this bloke turns up to check out his new land, have Agatha send him away with his tail between his legs."

"Okay." She bit her lip. "Is it okay if Jordan comes over this morning? The nursery is closed for an inset day and he wants to do some work—otherwise known as colouring—here in the office. He would have asked last night, but sent a text instead."

TJ raised an eyebrow. "He's three. He can't write or read. And what's an inset day?"

"Okay, picky-picky. Aunt Agatha sent a text and

asked on his behalf. And inset is in-service training. Basically, the teachers get taught."

He smiled. "Sounds good. Ask her to bring in a picnic lunch for you, me, and Jordan. We'll take him to the park and picnic where you and I did the other day."

"He'd like that."

"Right." The kettle boiled and he picked it up. "Time to make some tea and toast. Then I'm off to the solicitors, and you can start work."

Zara touched his arm. "TJ, there's something I need to tell you…"

The phone rang. TJ grabbed it. "Hebron Stables, TJ Greggson speaking."

"TJ, it's Ben." His lawyer sounded remarkably chipper. "Can you come in now? I need to see those papers."

"Sure. See you in a few." TJ hung up. "Zara, we'll have to talk later. The lawyer wants me and the papers in his office now." He kissed her gently.

"It's important…"

"And I promise, later." He headed to the safe. "Now eat something before you start work."

Zara was in the middle of tidying the tack room when a car pulled up at the gates and blasted its horn. She shook her head. "Use the buzzer like everyone else," she muttered.

Jordan tugged her sleeve. "Who's that?"

She bit her lip. Her insides churned with nerves as the horn sounded again. "Someone called Mr. Impatient by the sounds of it. Shall we go and see?"

Jordan took her hand and they headed into the yard. "That's Gampa's car. Can I go and say hello?"

"Not right now." Zara picked him up and balanced him on her hip, moving swiftly into the office. She should have at least told TJ her father was the buyer. He'd never forgive her. Neither of them for that matter.

Aunt Agatha glanced up at her. "Your father…"

"I know. Keep Jordan here. I'll get rid of him." She hit the open gate button and headed into the yard. The black limo halted. A tall, brown-haired man got out. Zara sucked in a deep breath. *You can do this…*

"Zara."

"Hi, Dad."

"I'm here to see TJ Greggson. I now own this land."

"TJ isn't here. He's with his solicitor in town."

"He knew I was coming. And it's a little late for a lawyer. This is a done deal."

She glared pointedly at her father. "Some papers came to light last night that negate the court order allowing the sale of this land. So, whatever deal you concocted with Xavier is null and void."

Her father's face darkened. "*What?*"

"You heard. This place is off the market. Permanently. It can't be sold. Not even if you force TJ's hand as well."

Her father snarled and grabbed her arm, pulling her to

one side. "Now listen here, girlie. You were sent here to foreclose on this deal weeks ago. Instead you've been nothing but a stumbling block."

"I'm not letting you cheat TJ like you did all those others."

"Like you did."

"I've changed. No more. And I work here now."

Her father peered at her, then pulled back. "You love him. Don't bother denying it, girlie. You've fallen for another low-life stable hand."

Zara stuck her chin out. "He is nothing of the kind. And so what if I have. Yes, I love him. He's good with Jordan. He likes me. I'm happy for the first time since Daniel died. I won't let you ruin this like you did that."

"And I won't let you ruin a good business deal. This land is worth millions and it's mine."

"No, it's not!"

A car door slammed. Quick footsteps strode across towards them. "Can I help?" asked the voice she loved. "I'm TJ Greggson."

Her father dropped Zara's arm and held out a hand, suddenly all smiles. "I'm James Michaels, Tennant's Builders. I've come to inspect my land."

"Michaels?" TJ's eyes widened, his jaw dropping

The older man nodded. "I'm Zara's father. Didn't she tell you?"

"No, she did not." His head swivelled from the angry man to Zara. "Your father is behind the attempt to buy my land?"

"I tried to tell you earlier, but—" She broke off, her

face burning. She felt three inches tall, like a bug waiting to be stomped on by a giant. She'd known for weeks, had ample time to tell him, but hadn't. She deserved everything she was about to get.

"She's working for me. The plan was to get you to fall in love with her and sell, like she's done countless times all over the country in the past three years."

TJ's face turned to stone. His eyes darkened and his hand clenched. "Is this true?" Even his voice was gritty.

"I…"

"Is it?" he yelled.

"It's not what you think." Overcome by shame, tears in her eyes, Zara turned and fled to where Rumple stood tacked up, ready for his morning ride. She threw herself into the saddle, gathering the reins.

"Zara wait!" TJ called. "Helmet!"

She tugged on the reins. Rumple gathered his haunches, leapt over the fence and galloped up the field.

No, no, no, no, no. TJ stood bereft. His heart lay in pieces within the confines of a tight chest. A lump blocked his throat. Any hope for a future with Zara he'd had since the uplifting visit to the solicitor quashed.

"She didn't tell you?" James Michaels strident voice cut through the grief.

TJ had almost managed to forget the man stood there. He cleared his throat. "No, she didn't. She'd said she'd been working for you and hated it. And she'd quit. Just before we collected Jordan."

Mr. Michaels snorted derisively. "Then it was you with her. I thought as much."

"When she quit, your plan failed. So you...what...bribed my brother instead, with a fake court order and a huge sum of money?"

"It worked." A smug smile stole over Mr. Michaels's lips.

Anger and bile rose, the potent mix churning in TJ's stomach. "Unfortunately, your court order isn't valid. Zara found papers predating it, forbidding the use of the land for anything other than use as stables, forbidding the sale of said land. Apart from to me. And should either myself or my brother leave, we forfeit our inheritance. So all of this is mine. And I'm not selling."

"We'll see about that," the man threatened.

"My solicitor is currently contacting both yours and Xavier's lawyers. He's drawn up the necessary papers and is on his way to the court right now to have the sale negated. To put it bluntly, I win." He took a deep breath, anxious to go after Zara and put things right between them. "I would like you to get off my land. Now."

Jordan came running out waving a piece of paper. "Where's Mummy? I want to show her my drawing."

TJ picked him up, setting him on his hip. "I'm going to go and find her. She went riding without her hat."

Jordan's mouth opened wide. "That's naughty. Even I know that."

"I'm going to go and give it to her. I need you to stay

with Auntie Aggie and not leave her side for a second. Can you do that?"

Jordan nodded. "Hi, Gampa."

"Grandpa is just leaving." TJ glared at Mr. Michaels. "I suggest you get off my land before I call the police and have you arrested for trespassing."

"This isn't over."

"Then I look forward to seeing you again for round two."

"By the way, if she told you she loved you, bear in mind she only gains access to her inheritance *after* she gets married. So that would be why she's doing this."

TJ's stomach twisted and his heart stopped. Desperate to keep control on his shattered emotions, he carried Jordan inside and settled him behind the desk. "Agatha, I'm going after Zara. Make sure her father leaves. If he doesn't, call the cops."

"TJ?"

"I don't have time to explain. Keep Jordan away from him and make sure that man leaves." He paused. "One question. Zara's trust fund. Does she only get it when she's married?"

Agatha nodded. "Yeah. Why?"

"Nothing." TJ grabbed his riding hat and high-viz jacket and jogged outside. He'd been made a fool of for the last time.

TJ galloped Tog up the field, the horse's hooves tearing up the ground. Zara's helmet and high-viz jacket attached to his saddle.

If he knew Zara at all, she'd flee to her favourite spot. The high field overlooking the valley. They'd gone there several times over the past few weeks, both by horse and car. He doubted she'd have ridden the long way there, especially as she set off over the field to begin with. Worried prayers flew heavenward. He needed to find her, talk this out. He still loved her. Of course he did. That wasn't in doubt. He needed to know if she loved him or whether the proposal was all part of this elaborate scam, ruse, or whatever she and her father had cooked up between them. Or just a ploy to get ahold of her money?

Had she tricked Daniel the same way? Was he simply another in a long line of men?

Finally he spotted her on the path ahead, no longer galloping. Instead she had Rumple at a slow trot. He urged Tog on faster. "Zara! Slow down."

She glanced over her shoulder, hesitated, then pulled up Rumple, slowing to a walk.

TJ caught her, reining in Tog to match Rumple's pace. "I need a word."

She shook her head. Her face was red and blotchy.

He scowled. "Hat!" He handed her the helmet. "Even Jordan said you need it, now put it on."

She took the helmet and shoved it on her head, not doing it up.

He laid the high-viz jacket on her saddle. "Can we

179

talk?"

She wiped her arm over her face. "No point. It's over. He told you everything."

"I want to hear it from you." Despite his anger and frustration, TJ made an effort to keep his voice calm. "Did you betray me?"

"No..." A strangled sob erupted from Zara. "I'd never do that."

"He said you came here to seduce me. To report to him. Check out my land and force me to sell." His gut twisted, chest tightened. "I trusted you. I opened up to you in ways I haven't with anyone else, ever. I fell in love with you. I gave you my heart. I thought your proposal was genuine. But now I discover you only want to marry me to get access to your trust fund."

"That's not how it is."

Anger coursed through him. His fists tightened on the reins. "Then, tell me exactly how it is."

Zara dipped her face, unable to meet his searching gaze, compounding his worst fears. "I didn't tell him anything. I told you how to prevent the sale. I found that box containing the wills weeks ago—shortly after the house fire. I could have told him, but I didn't. I told you about them last night."

"Yeah, way too late. I could have stopped all this. Instead, he goes to Xavier, intent on revenge, because I helped you get your son away from him. His words not mine."

Zara straightened in the saddle. "Everything was under control. You'd stopped the sale. I didn't know he was going to be this conniving. Okay, yes, he sent me here. I told you that much on the train, that first day we met. But I didn't know it was your land until Aunt Agatha dropped you off at the stables. She told me not to hurt you."

TJ sucked in a deep breath. His whole body in turmoil, but yelling at each other wasn't solving anything. Maybe if he lowered his voice he'd get the whole story. "Look at me."

She turned slowly. Her eyes brimmed with tears.

"Oh, don't try the waterworks on me. It won't work. Have you any idea how angry I am with you, right now?"

Zara shrugged. She slid off Rumple and tied his reins to the fence. She pulled her hat off, letting it fall to her feet. "I love this place," she whispered. "I love you. I'd never hurt you."

He snorted. "Yeah, right. I thought we were friends. More than friends. I can't believe I was even considering your proposal. And speaking of which—is it true? That you only get access to your trust fund when you get married?"

Colour rose in her cheeks. "Yes, but that isn't why I proposed. I don't want the money."

"Then why?"

She shook her head and wiped her eyes. "Because I love you. But like I said, I know it's over."

He studied her for a few moments. "You know what stopped me from saying yes right off?"

Her eyes scanned his face. "What?"

"The prospect of losing the stables. Of having nothing to offer you or Jordan. And don't tell me all that money could buy me anything I wanted. Sure it'd buy a house, but I'd have no job, no prospects." He leapt to the ground and tied Tog beside Rumple. The two horses grazed, oblivious to the conflict around them.

He grabbed Zara's arm, holding her gently, but firmly. A million emotions crippled his insides, and he didn't know which of them to give into first. "Look at me, honey."

Slowly she raised her face, tear tracks evident on her cheeks.

"Your father is trying to get between us, even now. I want to know the truth about what you did for him."

"Can we sit?"

"Sure."

She plonked down on the grass and picked at a nail. Her teeth worried her bottom lip. "He paid me to date men whose property he wanted to buy and develop. Have dinner with them. Convince them to sell at lower than market price. He paid a private detective to follow me, have photos taken in case his offer was refused. The idea being he'd send the photos to the wives and use them as blackmail."

TJ studied her. "Are there photos of us?"

She shook her head. "No. The PI is a friend of mine. He told me what was going on and I persuaded him not to take any pictures. I hated every minute of it. Coming here, meeting you, seeing what you do, what you'd lose, put everything in perspective."

"Date, dinner…makes you sound like an escort."

Zara groaned. "That's what he wanted. But it was merely dinner and a conversation. I never slept with any of them, despite being told to or propositioned. Without Jesus in my life it would have been different, but He gave me another option. What Dad didn't realize was all they needed was the financial side of things explained better than Dad or his solicitor ever did. I hated every minute of it, longed to escape, but he held Jordan over me."

She twisted her hands in her lap. "I regret every minute of it. I never cared for any of them, no matter what Dad believes. But coming here? I really did fall in love with you. The thing about the trust fund…I don't care if I never see a penny of it."

"I see." TJ glanced sideways at her, and then turned away. He didn't know what to do. Heart and soul told him one thing, cool mind telling him something else entirely.

"Please don't look at me like that. I know it's over between us. I'll take Jordan and leave. No idea where. Aunt Agatha can return my uniform when it's clean."

He grabbed her hand. "Oh, no. I don't think so. You are not getting away that easily."

"What?" Confusion flickered in her eyes.

He cupped her face in both hands. "Those papers you found, regardless of when, can stop the sale of my land. My lawyer is working on it now." The new mobile in his pocket rang. "In fact, that's him now."

"How do you know?"

TJ fished the phone from his pocket. "Your aunt set it up with personalized ring tones. Hello, TJ Greggson speaking." He listened. "Thank you. Thank you so much. Can I make an appointment on Friday afternoon for all parties to come into your office? Yeah, a text is fine." He hung up and beamed.

"What?"

"The sale is null and void and has been stopped. It was illegal." He hugged her, joy replacing every negative emotion in his body. "And when Xavier walked out, he forfeited any rights to the land or money. It's all mine. Thank you. You saved the stables." He kissed her.

Zara closed her eyes, returning the kiss.

He broke off, holding her gaze. "Marry me."

"I thought you hated me."

"Hate is a strong word. Plus there is a fine line between love and hate. But I could never hate you." He kissed her again. "Marry me."

"I asked first..."

He cupped her face. "And now I'm asking."

"Yes." She kissed him. "What about Jordan? He comes with me, obviously."

TJ smiled. "I would be honoured to be his daddy or just stay as Unca Teej. It's up to him what he wants to call me." He pulled Zara to her feet. "Let's go back, via the road. It's slightly longer, and will give me time to work out how to break the news to Xavier and your dad. And I need to ask Jordan to marry me as well."

"Yes."

"Something else I need to do." He pulled out his

phone. "Change your name to Zara ICE will you?"

"ICE?"

"In case of emergency, as per post July 7 bombing instructions. So they know who to call in an emergency."

She smiled. "Then I shall make you TJ ICE in my phone." She paused. "Do I want to know what my ring tone is?"

His cheeks started to heat. "Umm, no."

She giggled. "Can't be any more embarrassing as you falling off a horse into a water jump in front of the entire community at last year's fayre."

TJ groaned. "Alicia told you."

"She did. But don't worry. I came off in the final of the show jumping at the world championship several years back. The horse stopped and I didn't. To add insult to injury, as well as being eliminated, I even got awarded points for bringing down the fence…and the horse didn't even touch it."

TJ roared with laughter. "I wish I'd seen that."

Zara blushed. "It's on the internet. You can search for it."

He kissed her forehead. "Oh, believe me, I will. Now, put on your helmet and jacket, and let's go home."

Zara rode Rumple as he walked back to the stables in front of TJ. The sun blazed down and she was sure it reflected off her high-viz jacket, making it shinier than usual. But that didn't matter. She could have been riding on air. TJ still loved her and wanted her, despite her not being totally honest with him. "I still can't quite believe you love me."

"And why not? Like you said the other day, we all have a past. All that matters from here on is you and me and that we are always completely honest with each other. Deal?"

"Sounds good to me. The gates are just up ahead."

"Good. I'm starving. Never did have breakfast after rushing out first thing like that."

She snorted. "And you moaned at me for not eating. Lunch is in the office with Jordan, assuming he hasn't eaten it all."

"Did you bring pies?"

"Of course I did." She glanced over her shoulder. "We could have a wedding pie instead of a cake."

TJ laughed. "Now, there's an idea."

Two motorbikes zoomed past them way too fast, spooking both horses and riders.

Rumple jumped to one side, and began spinning in a circle, tossing his head, ears forward. Tog did the same thing.

Zara gripped Rumple's reins firmly. "Hey!"

TJ reined Tog to a halt and glared after the bikers. "Slow down idiots! Zara, are you okay?"

She was still trying to control Rumple. "Yeah, I'm fine. Rumple not so much. Easy boy."

"Try to move him on," TJ told her. "If you drag out

the spook, it makes things worse."

She spoke calmly. "It's okay." She pulled gently on the reins and squeezed her thighs gently to keep him moving. "Let's go home. We're almost there, see?"

After what seemed like a lifetime, Rumple stopped turning and walked forward. He kept tossing his head, his ears twitching.

Zara patted his neck. "I know, total idiots, weren't they?"

Another car zoomed up behind them. "For Pete's Sake!" TJ yelled. "Slow down."

Startled again, Rumple dashed into the middle of the road.

As she struggled for control, Zara saw TJ wave his whip at the driver from the corner of her eye.

"Slow down!" he yelled.

The car slowed and stopped, putting on its hazard lights.

In a total panic, Rumple spun, not at all happy.

"Pull him back," TJ instructed. "Give him a kick on, tap him on the shoulder with your whip if need be."

"Come on boy." Zara clicked her tongue.

Another car zoomed around the corner on the wrong side of the road.

TJ waved at the driver. "STOP!"

Zara hauled on the reins and tried clicking again.

A flash of red filled her vision.

Screeching brakes echoed in the lane.

Then she was flying through the air as the car hit her and Rumple head on.

CHAPTER 13

EVERYTHING SLOWED.

Brakes squealed. Glass shattered, exploding outwards in slow motion. A sickening thud. A scream.

TJ wasn't sure if it was Zara or Rumple who screamed as both were tossed into the air, onto the car, before flying off onto the roadside.

TJ leapt off Tog, his heart pounding, stomach churning. He held Tog's reins tightly. "Easy, girl." His training kicked in. DR-ABC. Danger, response, airway, breathing, call 999.

Not letting go of Tog, he glanced over at Zara and Rumple. Neither were moving. Fear kicked the hornets' nest in his gut over. "Zara! Zara can you hear me, honey? Say something if you can."

A car door slammed shut. One of the passengers from

the first stationary car, a girl, ran over to him. The other headed towards the other car.

"Can I do anything?" the girl asked.

"Are you any good with horses?"

"I am," the girl said.

"Good. This is Tog. Take her reins and lead her to the stables up ahead on the right. Hit the intercom on the gate. Tell them there's been an accident and Zara and Rumple are down. Tell them you have Tog and I need Alicia and Gerry here now. You got all that?"

"Sure." She took the reins. "Hello, Tog. Oh, such a gorgeous horse, aren't you? Let's go this way." She clicked and led Tog away from the accident scene.

"What can I do?" The bloke shifted from one foot to the other. "The driver of the other car is trapped"

"Call 999. We need everything out here ASAP." TJ moved to Zara's side. "Zara, honey, can you hear me?" He checked her airway and breathing. He didn't dare move her, not even into the recovery position. Blood seeped from her ear. The silk on her hat was torn—did it hide a crack? *Thank you, Lord, she was wearing it.*

He got up and moved over to Rumple. "Hey, Rumple." The horse had gone from flat out to lying on his side, the half up position most horses sleep in. Rumple shook his head. His eyes were wild. Obviously scared silly, he snorted, huffed and tried to get up.

TJ held his reins and stroked his nose. "Easy, boy. Rumple, stay down a minute."

The bloke handed TJ the phone.

TJ sighed in exasperation and took it. "Yes, we need

police, fire, ambulance and a vet. I have a collision between a rider, horse and a speeding idiot in a car. Vicarage Road, Hebron Stables. The road is completely blocked in both directions. The rider is critical and the idiot is still trapped in his car." He gave the bloke the phone back. "Hold Rumple's reins, don't let him get up."

"How?"

"Hold the reins short, like this, and he won't move."

"Okay. Where are you going?"

"Back to Zara."

Zara's eyes fluttered open. Why was she sleeping in the middle of the road? Had she fallen off the horse or something? She tried rolling over. Pain shot through every part of her. She moaned.

TJ appeared by her side, his cool hand against her face. He took off his helmet, laying it beside her. "No, no, honey, don't move. I need you to keep completely still." His hands slid around her neck, keeping her head immobile.

"What happened?"

"Car hit you. Help is on the way."

"Where's Rumple?"

"He's over there. He's okay."

Running footsteps echoed, stopping by her legs.

"What happened?" came Alicia's voice.

"Zara and Rumple got hit by the idiot in that car over there. Haven't had time to check the driver myself, but he's not going anywhere judging from the state of the damage. Alicia, can you call Kyle out for Rumple? I need you to check Tog over. She wasn't hurt, but she's bound to be in shock. Un-tack her, put her in a stall with hay and water. And keep Agatha and Jordan away, will you? I also need Matt out here with the horse box to get Rumple back to the stables or wherever Kyle wants him taken. Gerry, I need you to sit with Rumple. The car hit him full on. Don't let him get up or move until the vet gets here."

"Sure. Agatha's keeping Jordan in the office. She wants to be informed the minute you know anything."

Zara tried an experimental deep breath, and wished she hadn't. She whimpered. "I need to check Rumple. Make sure he's okay." Stabbing pain knifed her as she moved.

"Shh. Calm down." TJ's fingers stroked her cheeks. "You have the memory of a fish, honey. I just asked Gerry to take care of Rumple."

Sirens wailed in the distance.

"Stay down, Rumple, you're okay," Gerry said.

A moan tore through Zara as she tried to get up, pain searing through every nerve.

"Lie still," TJ told her, increasing his grip on her neck. "You may have hurt your neck. You've definitely hurt your legs, so you can't walk even if you did get up."

She bit her lip in an effort to keep quiet. Her cheeks were wet. Was she crying? Why did everything seem so far away? "Where…"

TJ's fingers wiped away the tears. "It'll be okay."

Several police cars, two ambulances, fire engines came to a halt around them. No sirens now, just lights.

"Why no sirens?" she managed.

"So we don't spook Rumple any more than he already is."

"TJ?" Kyle appeared next to her. "What happened? I came to see Pipkin and found Alicia waiting for me by the gate."

"Rumple got hit full on by a car. I don't know how badly hurt she is. Tog's in the yard. She's unhurt, but can you check her anyway before you leave?"

Two booted feet and green legs appeared in Zara's field of vision. "Hi, my name's Ian. This is Jess. Can you tell me your name?"

"Zara."

"Nice name. Same as Princess Anne's daughter. You came off the horse?"

"Knocked off. Couldn't get out of the way, Rumple was spooking."

The other paramedic glanced at TJ. "Are you hurt?"

"No. And I didn't move her."

"Good. Jess, can you get the spinal board, neck collar, saline and morphine. Zara, can you tell me where it hurts?"

"Legs, neck, stomach. Need to see Rumple." She moved, only to cry out in agony.

"No you don't. The vet is with the horse and the only place you're going is the hospital. Are you allergic to anything?"

"Idiot drivers that hit horses, penicillin, and aloe vera."

Ian chuckled. "Right you are."

Zara raised her eyes to TJ. "Your hands are cold."

"That's because I have a warm heart." His eyes glistened.

"Are you crying?"

He blinked. "Nope."

"Just checking. Your phone is playing the Ride of the Valkyries."

He grinned. "That's your aunt's ring tone. Told you, I have a different tone for everyone."

The other paramedic returned and knelt by Zara's head. "Can I put this collar on you?"

TJ let go of Zara's neck and answered his phone. "Agatha, calm down. The paramedics are with her now. She's awake, but not making much sense as she's in a lot of pain."

"Hey, I resemble that remark... or is it resent?" she whispered.

"I'm going to put an IV in your arm to give you some fluids and pain meds," Ian told her. "I need you to keep still for me."

"Which hospital are you taking her to?" TJ asked.

"The RBH."

"The Royal Berks," TJ said into the phone. "Get her father to meet me there. No, I'd like you to stay with Jordan. I'll call you as soon as I know anything, I promise." He pocketed the phone.

Zara blinked hard. "I can't move."

"That would be the splints I put on your legs to keep them still. You've dislocated your knee. Normally I'd put it back in, but I want the doctor to have a look first. Just in case it's broken as well." Ian checked the IV. "Can I have some help here, please?"

Four fire fighters appeared in an instant.

"I need to log roll her onto the spinal board, and then lift her onto the trolley. Possible spinal injury, so very gently does it, lads."

Zara closed her eyes and moaned as she was manoeuvred onto the board, then lifted.

"He hit her head on, speeding on the wrong side of the road like a maniac." TJ's voice came from a distance. He must be talking to the police. "There's a CCTV camera right there. I need to go with her."

She tried to reach up, but they must have tied her down. "TJ…"

"I'm coming, Zara." He climbed up into the ambulance and perched on the seat where she could see him. "I'm not leaving you."

"I'll do the paperwork on the way, Jess. Blues and twos all the way. Step on it. Call it in and tell them we need the trauma team outside waiting for us."

Everything swam. "I don't feel so good. TJ…"

His voice drifted even further away. "Zara? Zaraaaa….."

CHAPTER 14

ZARA OPENED HER EYES AS the shifting movements stopped. The ambulance doors opened. Light streamed in, making her squint.

TJ smiled. "She's back with us."

"Not before time."

She groaned as the trolley was lifted from the ambulance to the floor.

"Straight into resus, please." A man in blue scrubs stood over her. "What have we got?"

"Quinn, this is Zara Michaels, twenty-eight." Ian spoke as they wheeled her inside at full speed. "Out riding, both she and horse were hit head-on by a speeding driver. She's complaining of neck and stomach pain. She passed out in the ambulance, but woke as we pulled up. She has a dislocated left knee. Query pelvis,

195

spine, and right leg. She's allergic to idiot drivers, penicillin and aloe vera. The helmet appears damaged. We didn't remove it."

The tall, extremely good-looking man with blond hair shot her a dashing smile. "Hello, Zara. I'm Quinn Southgate, one of the trauma surgeons here. How are you doing?"

Drugged up to the eyeballs and floating six feet above this trolley, which is weird 'cos I'm strapped to it is what she wanted to say. What actually came out was, "Need to find Rumple and Teej."

"Rumple is her horse," Ian explained. "I'm assuming Teej is TJ. He came in with her."

The handsome doctor nodded. "I'll find out about the horse, but first I need to make sure you're okay. Let's move her onto the bed on three."

Zara cried out as they moved her. Even though she was sure they didn't drop her from a great height, it sure seemed like they had. A light flashed in her eyes, monitors started to bleep. She squeezed the doctor's fingers when he asked. Scissors started to cut off her clothes. She wanted to stop them. This was the only pair of jodhpurs that really fitted properly and had cost a small fortune from the riding shop on the outskirts of the village.

She raised a hand, peering at the needle sticking out of it. "What's this for?"

"That's for the fluids and pain meds." The doctor gently seized her hand and placed it back on the bed. "I want to send you for a CT scan and some x-rays, check your head, neck, and spine before we take off the helmet and collar."

A loud voice boomed from across the room. "I'm her father. I have a right to see her."

Zara closed her eyes. He was the last person she wanted to see.

"Mr. Michaels," a female voice said. "You'll have to wait until the doctor has finished examining her."

"Want TJ," Zara whispered.

"Is TJ your boyfriend?" the doctor asked.

"Fiancé. We're getting married."

"Congratulations."

"Really dizzy…feel sick." Everything swam and she shut her eyes tight. She couldn't be sick, not strapped down like this, she'd choke. She sucked in several deep, painful breaths. After a moment the nausea passed.

"Call CT. I need to get her up there stat. Then get her to x-ray."

"TJ…"

A rustling sounded at her side. "Right here, honey. Can I have a minute, doctor?"

"Thirty seconds. We need to move quickly here."

A hand slid into hers, but she didn't open her eyes. "You'll be okay, love. I'll look after your dad while the doctors take care of you. I need to talk to him, remember?"

"He won't give…"

His lips brushed against her forehead. "See you soon." His hand left hers.

No longer grounded, Zara let the darkness take her.

Anything was better than the constant spinning and floating.

Having given the police a statement, TJ found Zara's father sitting in the waiting area. He appeared as bad as TJ felt. Like something had broken, been ripped from him, and could never be replaced or repaired. TJ slumped into the chair next to him. "The nurse said she'd call me once Zara is back from CT. Do you fancy a coffee?"

Mr. Michaels hesitated. "I shouldn't leave…"

"They'll call. It could be a while."

"Okay." He stood and followed TJ out of the ED and around to the main entrance. "Is there no access to the rest of the hospital from here?"

TJ shook his head. "No. In some ways it's silly, but in other ways it protects the rest of the patients." He paused. "Thinking about it, there probably is, at least for the doctors, so they can reach the other departments."

"Makes sense."

TJ bought two coffees and they found a table overlooking the entrance to the ED. Rows of ambulances parked outside.

"How's the horse?"

"I'm still waiting for Alicia to ring, but he was pretty badly cut up. The car came out of nowhere on the wrong side of the road. It went straight into them." He closed his eyes, seeing the accident happen again in slow motion.

"I see."

TJ buried his head in his hands. "Everything is such a mess. We'd talked about what you said. She said she'd been sent by you to seduce me like she'd done loads of times to other men on your behalf. She told me why she quit. You know why you never saw any photos? She'd paid the photographer not to take them."

Mr. Michaels shook his head. "That's Zara. Always goes her own way no matter what."

"She fell in love with me, couldn't see me as another job. And she loves the stables."

Mr. Michaels scowled.

TJ pushed down what he wanted to say. The man was in shock after all. But second thoughts, if he didn't say it, no one would. "Zara deserves better from you," he said, probably more bluntly that he should do. "You're her father. You are meant to stand by her, pick her up when she falls and care for her. Not act like her…" He let out a deep breath, changing his mind. "If I ever have any kids, I hope I do right by them."

Mr. Michaels frowned. "I've spoken to my lawyer. He emailed a copy of that will to my phone. I have withdrawn my offer for your land. I regret any unnecessary distress my actions caused you."

TJ swallowed. Fact was the man had inadvertently caused the accident. If Zara hadn't gotten upset, she'd never have ridden off like that. They'd never have been on the road, which was his idea for the route home.

They'd have been safe in the park having a picnic lunch with Jordan. But doubtless her father was also well aware of the consequences of his sending Zara here and of turning up the way he had that morning.

TJ's phone rang. "Hello…yeah, we'll be right there." He hung up. "Zara's back from CT. The doctor wants to see us." He stood. "You should know that I'm listed as her next of kin in her phone. I proposed, actually she did first, but we're engaged. I intend to marry her, no matter what. We're not interested in the money from her trust fund."

"And Jordan? Kids are expensive."

"Kids need love and stability far more than possessions and money. Jordan is a cute kid. He calls me Unca Teej, says I read 'betterer than mummy' unquote, and I'd be proud to call him my son. Whether I remain Unca Teej or become Dad will be up to him."

He hurried back to the ED, Mr. Michaels trailing behind. The trauma doctor stood waiting for them in reception.

"How is she?"

"Her neck isn't broken, nor is her spine. She has several cracked ribs. Her right ankle is fractured, her left knee dislocated. She's bleeding internally, so we're taking her up to theatre. I'll straighten her knee, fix her ankle and deal with the bleeding once she's under anaesthetic. She'll be on Heygroves Ward once she's out of recovery. Give me four hours or so then head up there. She's already being prepped, so you can't see her I'm afraid."

"You're doing the surgery?" TJ wasn't sure he'd heard right. "I thought you were an ED doctor."

"Trauma surgeon. I go where I'm needed. So it's Mr. Southgate, rather than Dr. Southgate. It's a long-standing tradition that surgeons are called Mr. or Ms rather than Dr."

"All that training to lose the doctor," TJ said. "May I pray for you before you take her up?"

The doctor smiled. "I'd like that. Thank you."

TJ prayed aloud, not caring who else was listening. He prayed for Zara, the skill of the medics treating her, and then added a bit for all the other patients currently in the ED. He finished. He hoped it made more sense than his saying grace had that time.

"Thanks so much," the surgeon said, and then headed back inside resus.

TJ slumped into one of the orange chairs. "Now what? Xavier needs the money and I can't give it to him. He'll hate me because I sabotaged the sale."

Mr. Michaels sat beside him. "No, you didn't. That will you found proves you were right."

"Actually, Zara found them. They were buried in a cupboard they should never have been in."

"Sounds to me like they were hidden."

TJ jerked. "You think Xavier did it deliberately? To force my hand? He couldn't be diabolical enough to destroy them, but still made it so I couldn't find them?"

"It's possible. Anyway, I've stopped the transfer of any funds he was expecting. He can get mad at the both of us." Mr. Michaels paused. "It appears I was wrong, about a lot of things. This has put everything into perspective for me. I could lose her without ever really understanding her."

"We both could."

"She told me how much this place means to her. I'd like to see it. Would you mind taking me over to the stables? Show me why Zara loves it here so much."

TJ nodded. "Okay. We were on our way to talk to you, Mr. Michaels. To ask your blessing on the wedding, and now..." he broke off. "I guess we just trust God to work this out."

Mr. Michaels inclined his head. "If you say so. I'll follow you. Parking here is daylight robbery."

TJ parked in his usual spot at the stables. He still felt sick, as if he'd left his heart and soul—the very best part of him—back in town in surgery. He prayed she'd wake up, that she'd recover. He couldn't lose her. Without her, the hard-won battle over the stables would be in vain.

Agatha ran out to meet him, before he was even out of the car. "How is she?"

"She's in surgery." He climbed out of the vehicle and glanced around at the other staff surrounding him. "She's got a fractured ankle, dislocated knee, internal bleeding. We won't know anything for a few hours. How's Rumple?"

"The vet sedated him," Alicia said. "But he'll be fine,

just cuts and bruises. Nasty cut on his leg will need dressing every day for a bit. Tog and Pipkin are both fine. Kyle promised you a nice big bill."

"I bet he did. Add it to the list of invoices I can't pay."

Jordan dashed out of the office. "Unca Teej. Did you find Mummy?"

TJ scooped him up. A waft of Zara's perfume caught him unawares. "Hiya, squirt... I did." He glanced at Mr. Michaels. "There's been an accident. Mummy is in the hospital. The doctors and nurses are taking care of her and will make her better."

Jordan's bottom lip trembled. "Want Mummy."

TJ hugged him. "So do I. But we'll go see her later on."

"Promise?"

"Yes. And we'll record a video of you on my phone to show her as well. Now, how about we show Grandpa the horses? Then you can make Mummy a huge get-well card with stuff in the classroom."

Jordan perked up a tad. "All those glittery bits?"

TJ nodded. "Auntie Aggie can get all the glittery bits and sticky bits out for you."

Agatha lifted an eyebrow. "Really? *All* the glittery bits."

TJ nodded. "And Alicia can put them all away and clear up the mess."

Alicia groaned. "Thanks, boss. Not like I have any other work to do."

"You're welcome." TJ swung Jordan to the ground

and clasped his hand. "So, what do we show Grandpa first?"

TJ spent two hours showing Zara's father around the stables, explaining what they did. Jordan was with Agatha in the classroom, drawing and making about fifty cards for Zara.

"I can see why she loves it here." Mr. Michaels leaned on the fence, watching the horses huddle under the giant table. "Love the shelter."

"That was Zara's idea. After the tree was destroyed in the storm, right along with my home, she came up with the table to get around planning regs for sheltering the horses."

Mr. Michaels smiled. "Sounds like her. She never was happy unless she was around horses. I should never have made her give up riding the way I did. I don't think she'll ever forgive me for that."

"She might. She doesn't hold grudges."

"What's up with Pipkin?"

"Colic. Zara was up most of the night with him." TJ rested his foot on the bottom rail of the fence. "She loves it here. I love it here. I simply can't see a way out."

"What do you mean?"

"The insurance won't cover the rebuild of the house—though they might now the sale has been halted. Xavier needs money and the bank won't give either of us a loan. He has forfeited any rights he had to this place, and even if I wanted to help him out financially, I can't. I'm struggling to makes ends meet as it is, right now."

"Not necessarily." Mr. Michaels eyed him. "What was the original land valuation?"

"Half a million. So Xavier would, in theory, get half of that."

"You'll have access to her trust fund so you can use that to pay off the bills and whatever else you need it for."

TJ straightened. "I don't see how I'll have access to her trust fund? It's hers."

Mr. Michaels shook his head. "Access goes to her husband. Only she doesn't know that. That groom of hers found out. It's why he wanted to marry her. I never had the heart to tell her."

TJ let out a long, slow breath. "Well, it's not why I want to marry her, I can tell you that. I love your daughter, more than life itself. And I'm not using her money to pay off my brother."

Mr. Michaels turned his back on the fence and looked out over the partly-fixed house. "Okay. How about I give you and Zara the half a million for this place as a wedding present? I'll also get my blokes to fix that up, however you and Zara want it. Along with any other improvements you want done."

TJ stood, stunned. "You serious? Why?"

"Very. You and Zara love this place. And it's an investment. You legally own the whole place. You don't owe your brother a penny, but should you want to give him some of this money, you could do. Or you could put it all into this place. It'll be my grandson's after all, one day."

Alicia trotted over to them. "TJ, Xavier is on the office phone."

His brother was the last thing on his mind. "Tell him to get off it before he breaks it," TJ snapped.

"Hah, Funny. He said to tell you he's not happy. He's on his way down. Did you want to speak to him?"

TJ's mobile rang. "One minute. Hello?"

"Mr. Greggson, its Sister Tyler from Heygroves Ward. Zara is back with us. She's a little groggy still, but asking for you."

"Thank you. Her father and I will be right in." He hung up and shrugged at Alicia. "Tell Xavier I'm on my way to the hospital to visit my critically injured fiancé, and I'll see him when he gets here. Is he driving?"

"Flying."

"Okay, I'm not going to ask how he can afford that at a moment's notice. Never mind how he got a seat on a plane. Tell him I'm living in a caravan as the house isn't safe. He can find a hotel in town if a caravan isn't good enough for him." He broke off. That sounded harsher than he wanted. "Just tell him I'll see him when he gets here."

When he got to the hospital, Zara was sleeping. He sat by the bed and glanced at the clock. Just after five. He'd sit here as long as it took.

Zara gripped TJ's hand tightly, never wanting to let it go again. She had no idea how long she'd been sleeping, but the clock on the wall told her it was almost eight in the evening. She ran her tongue over cracked and sore lips. "How long was I out?"

"A while."

"Have you been here all the time?"

"I went back home for a bit, but I've been sat here for several hours now, listening to you snore."

"How's Rumple?"

TJ smiled. "I'm fine, thank you, honey."

She pressed her lips together. "I can see that. That's why I asked after Rumple."

"Rumple's doing okay. Kyle patched him up, and he's sleeping right now. Few cuts and bruises, but Kyle says he'll mend just fine. Though he isn't going to want to go on the road for a while."

"Neither do I." She glanced up, seeing her father standing behind TJ. "Hi, Dad."

"Hey, baby girl. How you doing?"

"Sore. I'm sorry I disappointed you."

Her father sat on the bed and took her other hand. "TJ and I had a long talk while you were in surgery. He berated me about the way I'd treated you and rightly so. After your mum died, I tried hard to be both parents. I had your best interests at heart, believe me. But she wouldn't like what I made you do."

Zara couldn't believe she was hearing this. Her father never admitted he was wrong about anything. She gripped his hand hard. "I wanted you on my side."

"I always am. Just not very good at showing it." Her father glanced at TJ, then back at her. "TJ tells me you're getting married."

She nodded, wincing as pain coursed through her neck and chest. "Not for the trust fund money either."

Her father smirked. "Just as well. Because that won't be yours."

She frowned. "I don't understand."

TJ brushed his fingers over the bruise on her forehead. "That, evidently, becomes mine. But as far as I'm concerned, it's your money. I'll simply transfer it to your bank account."

"You have a good man in TJ," her father said. "My lawyer got hold of me earlier. The legal documents say TJ owns the whole stables outright and can't be sold."

Zara tried not to roll her eyes. That was her father to a tee. Change the subject back to business.

"The land is worth half a million. I'm going to give you both the money as a wedding present."

She flicked her eyes from her father to TJ.

TJ grinned. "That's if you still want to marry me. We can use some of the money to give Xavier. We owe him nothing, but he's still my brother, even if he is a huge pain in the backside most of the time. That's if it's okay with you."

"More than okay." She tried smiling, but even the slight effort turned into a groan of pain.

TJ leaned in and kissed her gently. "But you need to rest up before we start making wedding plans. Jordan has made you dozens of get well soon cards." He pulled one from his pocket. "He's planning on bringing the rest tomorrow."

Zara stared at the card, tears springing to her eyes. *Get Well Mummy, I Miss You* was written on the front.

"He dictated the message to Agatha. But inside, look..." He helped her open the card. It was splashed with kisses and a huge backwards J. "He did that all by himself."

"Oh..."

TJ gently wiped the tears that streaked her grazed and bruised cheeks. "He also left you a video message. We sent it to your phone. Want to hear it?"

"Yeah. It's in my locker, if it's not broken."

"Well the message said it was delivered, so hopefully it's not too smashed. Otherwise I'll play it on mine, I haven't deleted it yet." TJ pulled the handset from Zara's locker. "What's your code?"

"My birthday."

"That's not helpful or sensible."

"1708," she said, trying not to smile as smiling hurt.

TJ chuckled. "Guessing that's the seventeenth of August, rather than January seventh, 2008. Either that or you're very attractive for a woman of four hundred and something." He opened the message and held the phone in front of her.

The video showed TJ and Jordan. "Okay, Jordan, say hi to Mummy."

"Hi Mummy. When you coming home? 'Cos I miss you this much." Jordan's arms flew wide, knocking TJ in the face. "Unca Teej says he'll read to me every night. Love you."

Zara sobbed and traced a finger over the phone screen. "Love you too, little bug."

Someone in blue scrubs came over to the bed and picked up her notes. He flicked through them, and then smiled at her. "Hi, Zara. How are you doing?"

"Okay."

"Are you still on duty, Mr. Southgate?" TJ asked.

"On my way home. I wanted to check on Zara before I left. May I examine you quickly?"

She nodded. TJ and her dad left as the doctor closed the curtains around the bed.

A few minutes later, the doctor signed the notes and opened the curtains. "I will see you in the morning. If you need more pain relief overnight, let the nurses know."

"Thank you."

TJ moved closer to the bed. "Your Dad has headed back to Agatha's to help put Jordan to bed. I thought I might sit here with you for a bit longer, until they kick me out."

"How will you get home?"

"We brought both cars this time."

She managed a tiny smile. "Read me to sleep. Show me why you're a better reader than I am."

TJ whipped out his violet reading glasses and settled them on his nose. "Once upon a time…" He broke off with a smile. "Only kidding." He tugged his phone from his pocket. "I can actually read this thing now, rather than having to use the voice app." He pulled up his favourite psalm and began to read.

CHAPTER 15

Two Months Later…

ZARA GLANCED DOWN AT HER left hand. The sparkling engagement diamond she wore would soon be joined by a gold wedding band. She and TJ had picked out matching rings. The summer fayre had been combined with a wedding and reception and delayed until August nineteenth. That way her ankle had healed, as had her knee. They'd invited all their friends, family as well as stable staff and clients. And of course, all the locals had turned up for the fayre as usual.

Including Quinn Southgate, her surgeon, who incidentally attended the same church she and TJ did.

Zara gazed over the yard and fields. Several stalls sold seemingly everything under the sun. There was a bouncy castle, pony rides, apple bobbing, and hook-a-duck—with a prize given for each duck caught. The house was almost finished. At least they could live in it, so she and TJ wouldn't be spending their wedding night in the caravan.

White ribbons flew on every fence and post. Pots of confetti stood ready for three o'clock.

She peered over at the grotto and grinned at the sight of her husband dressed as a cowboy, offering rides on his bull—a dressed up hobby horse, or 'gablet horse' as Jordan called it.

She made her way over to him, still slightly cautious creeping along without the crutches.

TJ strode out to meet her. "How are you doing?"

"I think we're crazy to do this and get married on the same day."

"Me too, but it's what we both decided, and I wouldn't want it any other way." He tweaked her nose. "Besides, your sister said Zara's follies were almost world famous by now."

She giggled. "Did she now? Anyway, I'll go get changed as it's almost three. Aunt Agatha brought my dress over. Please tell me you're not getting married in a cowboy outfit."

He laughed. "Nope. My suit is in the caravan. And there's Xavier waving at me. Better go."

Zara nodded. "Kim is doing the same." She sighed. "Those two seriously need to get together and move to Scotland."

TJ laughed wickedly. "Then let's match-make all

afternoon." He paused, and then pointed. "What is your
aunt carrying?"

Zara laughed. "That, my love, is our wedding pie."

TJ roared with laughter. "Seriously? I thought you
were kidding?"

"Nope. Bottom layer is scotch. Second is macaroni.
Top is strawberry. There is a proper cake as well, I
promise."

He gave her the same look as Jordan did sometimes
when he thought she was speaking utter nonsense. "Then
I guess we have to be ultra-careful cutting it."

She kissed his nose. "We will."

TJ wrapped his arms around her and kissed her, one
of those mind-blowing kisses that transported her
elsewhere.

She opened her eyes and pulled back as someone
coughed. "Can I get you something for that cough,
Kim?"

"There'll be plenty of time for that mushy stuff later.
You need to get changed."

Jordan galloped over. "Can I ride the pony now,
Mummy?"

TJ snatched him up. "After your mummy and I get
married you can have as many rides as you like. Right
now, you need to put your new outfit on."

Jordan's eyes widened. "Cow…"

TJ clamped a hand over his mouth. "Shh… Secret,
remember?"

Zara grinned as Kim dragged her to the house. "No
more secrets," she called over her shoulder.

"After this, no more. Promise."

Zara slid her white stocking-clad feet into thick socks, before pulling on her knee high white riding boots. She'd bought these in the hope she'd be able to wear them. Worst case scenario would have been one riding boot and a load of bandages over the horrid Velcro support boot she'd been forced to wear. Either way she intended to wear these boots several times to get her money's worth.

Kim shook her head and stuck her hands on her hips. "I can't believe you're riding a horse in that dress. Aren't you afraid you'll ruin it?"

Zara ran her hands over the layers of white lace. The dress fitted tightly to her waist, where it then flowed out and down to the ground, a three-foot train trailing behind her. "I'm simply grateful it isn't raining. Or cold." She rubbed her bare arms, pretending to shiver.

Aunt Agatha laughed. She fitted the veil to Zara's head, careful not to displace the perfectly positioned curls. "Just wish you'd wear a helmet."

Zara groaned. "It's a gentle walk, with someone either side of the horse. No more than five feet. What could possibly go wrong?" She winked. "Besides, I am so *not* getting married with helmet hair."

Her father tapped on the door, sticking his head around the corner at the same time. "Are you ready?"

Zara nodded, standing and swishing from side to side to make the dress puff out a little. "Will I do?"

Her dad hugged her. "You look amazing. I don't think I've ever been prouder."

"Really?"

He nodded. "I know you've done some rash things in your life, but this isn't one of them."

She smiled and gathered her skirts. Her father wasn't exactly a changed man, but he'd tempered a lot since the accident. She liked the new man. "I don't want to keep him waiting."

Kim smoothed down her red dress. "How long has this place been licensed as a wedding venue?"

"About a year apparently...and we're the first wedding. Which is quite appropriate." She headed out into the sunshine.

Pipkin stood waiting for her. A white side-saddle, matching white bridle with bells adorned him. Someone had even plaited white ribbons into his tail. She patted his nose. "You are one handsome horse, fella, you know that."

"Why not have a carriage?" Kim tried again.

"Because I'm a rider not a driver." She gasped as her father swung her up on Pipkin's back. She gathered the reins. She could see TJ waiting at the top of the aisle. Jordan stood beside him, but as soon as he saw his mum, he tore across the yard toward her.

Zara laughed. Jordan's outfit was a perfect miniature replica of the outfit TJ sported a few minutes earlier—right down to the checked shirt, chaps, and sheriff's badge.

Her father boosted him up, and placed him in front of her.

"Hey, little bug."

"You're pretty, Mummy."

Zara smiled and tugged his miniature seven-gallon hat straight. "And you look like a proper cowboy."

Music began playing, and Zara clicked to Pipkin. "Walk on."

At one point, she doubted she'd ever get back on a horse again. And yet, here she was, riding towards her groom on the land they now both owned.

TJ beamed, glowing with love as she reached his side. His hands encircled her waist as he lifted her down. He whispered. "Can we skip to the kissing part now?"

Zara laughed. "All good things…"

Jordan stood between her and TJ.

TJ knelt beside him and caught hold of his hands. "Jordan, I have something very important to ask you. In a minute, I'm going to marry your mummy. She'll become Mrs Greggson."

"She won't be Michaels like me anymore?" Jordan asked.

TJ shook his head. "I'll give her a ring and that changes her name. But what I want to ask you is…" He reached into his pocket and pulled out the necklace he and Zara had chosen. "This is a St. Joseph medallion. He's the patron saint of fathers. I'd really like to be your daddy. If you don't want to, I'm still happy to remain Unca Teej."

Jordan eyed him seriously. "Will I have your name, as well?"

TJ nodded.

Jordan threw his arms around TJ's neck. "Yes. Yes, you can be my daddy."

Zara blinked back the tears, as TJ dropped the chain around Jordan's neck, and then hugged him tightly, his eyes also glistening.

TJ rose, not letting go of Jordan. His tears turned to a chuckle as Jordan turned to all the people gathered and yelled. "I'm getting a daddy!"

Zara seized TJ's hand. "Shall we?"

TJ nodded, his face beaming. "Yes, let's."

Glossary

Hack – an equestrian term meaning riding a horse for light exercise, at an ordinary pace, over a road or track.

Best of British – good luck

Shedload – an awful lot of something

Japanese car parts – a play on words. Cats and dogs mean lots of rain. Cats and dogs become dats and cogs, which become Datsun cogs hence Japanese car parts.

Stair rods – spindles which are part of traditional British bannisters. Long and straight – like torrential rain.

Trolley – shopping cart

Work top – kitchen counter

Schtum – means to be silent or keep quiet about something.

Scotch Pie recipe

Ingredients:
Filling
600g/1lb 5oz mutton/lamb mince
¼ teaspoon mixed herbs
5 tablespoon gravy or stock
Salt and pepper
Hot water crust pastry
½ teaspoon salt
120g/4¼oz lard
360g/12½oz plain flour
1 free-range egg yolk, beaten, for glaze

Method
Preheat - oven to 200C/400F/Gas 6.
Line - baking tray with baking parchment. Cut four strips of greaseproof paper, about 2ins deep and 10ins long, to wrap around the pies. You'll also need four pieces of string to secure the paper.
Filling - Mix all the ingredients together in a bowl and season. Work the liquid into the meat, divide into four portions and mould into balls. Refrigerate while you make the pastry.

Pastry - heat 160ml/5½fluid ounces of water, salt and lard in a saucepan until just boiling. Tip flour in a mixing bowl, add hot liquid and mix with a spoon. Once cool enough to handle, tip onto a floured surface and knead until you have a smooth dough.

Assembly - Cut off a quarter of the pastry and set aside. Divide the remaining dough into four equal balls. Roll out each ball to a 7in circle, about ¼in thick. Roll out the remaining pastry and cut out four circular lids, 4ins in diameter.

Place a ball of filling on each large circle of pastry. Gather the pastry around the meat and bring up the sides to form the shape of a pork pie. Stretch pastry so it comes above the meat by around 1¾in. Dampen the edges of the pies with water and press the lids on top of the filling. Seal the edges together using your fingers. Wrap a strip of greaseproof paper around each pie and secure with string to make sure the pie holds its shape when cooking.

Put the pies on baking tray. Cut a steam hole in the centre of each. Brush with beaten egg yolk.

Rest – 30 minutes in fridge.

Bake - 35-40 minutes, or until golden-brown.

All that Glitters

Excerpt from Clare Revell's new book from Pelican Book Group's Pure Amore series

PETER STANMORE STOOD ON THE Olympic podium, the men's figure skating gold medal surprisingly heavy around his neck. From the speakers to one side of the ice rink, the United Kingdom national anthem played while the Union Flag fluttered over his head. *This is for you, Mum and Dad.* Tears pricked his eyes as he sang along. He'd watched ceremonies like this before and couldn't believe the number of athletes who shed tears during them, yet here he was doing the very same thing. Crying and smiling with overwhelming happiness and at the same time, in awe of what he'd just done.

It had to be the pinnacle of his career. Proof, if proof were needed, that God honours those who honour Him.

Peter had made a concerted effort never to compete on a Sunday, which resulted in him being dropped from teams or not even selected. Sundays were for God, not for skating and definitely not for competitions. And it seemed his faith and determination were now paying off. Just as it had for Eric Liddell decades before him.

Peter finally had the medal he'd craved, without having to compromise either his beliefs or his promise to the Lord along the way.

And the glory went to God, not him.

He waved as the anthem ended and posed for photos with the other medallists, including the obligatory kissing-the-medal picture that he'd never seen the point of before and still didn't now. As the cameras flashed around him, the 'if onlys' began to filter through his mind.

If only things were different.

If only Mum and Dad were here. His heart broke that they weren't here to share it with him. An accident had ripped his family apart just months before the Olympics, taking his parents from him and leaving him alone. He hoped that somehow they were watching him from heaven and shared in the mixed emotions that filled him.

If only Jill had been here to collect it with him.

His career had begun in pairs skating. He and Jill worked their way up to the nationals and just as they were about to make it big, he'd messed up completely. As a result he'd made a career decision he now wished desperately he could undo. He'd allowed himself to be persuaded the right hand path was better than the left. That meant leaving Jill behind, a decision he'd regretted every moment of every day since.

This should have been both of them, not just him. He needed to call her, to put things right, to try to atone.

Three hours later, he sat on the couch in the team hotel still trying to pluck up the courage to call Jill.

Winston Brown, one of the bobsleigh team, nudged him. "Hey, a bunch of us are going to celebrate your win with a bottle of soda and a game of darts. Coming?"

"Sure, why not." He grabbed his coat and followed them outside. It was snowing again and the wind turned the heavy flakes into a blizzard. As Peter stepped out onto the wooden decking, his foot slipped on the ice beneath him sending him flying to the floor. His ankle snapped with an audible crack as he landed.

Pain ricocheted as stars danced in front of his vision. For a long moment he wasn't sure if he would throw up or pass out. Either way, nothing made much sense. He closed his eyes, hoping the pain would just go away.

Sometime later he opened his eyes to find a doctor wearing surgical scrubs beside his bed. He remembered falling and vaguely remembered an ambulance, but that could have been a dream. The smell told him he was in hospital, and he was definitely awake. Wide awake. He glanced down at his legs, but his vision was obscured by a screen. His stomach plummeted. "Doctor, what have I done? And please, don't sugarcoat it with platitudes. I need to know."

"OK, Mr. Stanmore. When you fell, you shattered your ankle. So we had to operate to screw your ankle back together. The metal pins will need a mention in your passport—I'll give you a letter for that. You'll be able to walk, possibly without a limp eventually, but I'm afraid your competing days are over. Your ankle just won't take the strain of the jumps and turns."

The bottom fell out of his world. The irony was not lost on him.

Only a few hours ago, he'd been on top of the world, literally. Now, he was at his lowest ebb. As the doctor left, Peter closed his eyes as the words of Psalm 31 filled his mind.

Be merciful to me, Lord, for I am in distress; my eyes grow weak with sorrow, my soul and body with grief. My life is consumed by anguish and my years by groaning; my strength fails because of my affliction, and my bones grow weak.

Jill Davenport picked up the local paper and put it on her mother's tray. Despite it being the previous day's news, her mother liked reading it over breakfast. Not that she remembered what she'd read, but it gave her something to do for a while. The headlines were once more dominated by the victorious Olympic team who, having won more medals at a Winter Games than any previous

British team, had visited both Downing Street and Buckingham Palace yesterday.

In the middle of the picture stood Peter Stanmore— the kid next door who grew up to be a friend, then more than a friend, and a skating partner...until the lights of stardom called him away, leaving her behind.

You can pick up a copy **Amazon US** or **Amazon UK**

Newsletter subscribe

I hope you enjoyed *Zara's Folly*. If you did, please consider leaving a review on Amazon. It doesn't have to be a long or wordy one. Even short, positive, "I really liked it" reviews count as they show the author they're appreciated and help point other readers to Christian fiction.

Thank you for reading.

If you'd like to receive information on new releases, new covers, and new writing projects, please email me at clarerevellauthor@revell124.plus.com and I can send you a link to the newsletter subscription. I promise I won't pass your email on to anyone else, you won't get millions of emails from me – four, maybe six a year if that.

About the Author

Clare lives in a small town just outside Reading, England with her husband, whom she married in 1992, their three children, and unfriendly mini-panther, aka Tilly the black cat. The household was joined by guinea pigs, Hedwig and Sirius fairly recently. Clare is half English and half Welsh, which makes watching rugby interesting at times as it doesn't matter who wins.

Writing from an early childhood and encouraged by her teachers, she graduated from rewriting fairy stories through fan fiction to using her own original characters and enjoys writing an eclectic mix of romance, crime fiction and children's stories. When she's not writing, she can be found reading, crocheting or doing the many piles of laundry the occupants of her house manage to make.

Her books are based in the UK, with a couple of exceptions, thus, the books contain British language and terminology and the more recent ones are written in UK English.

The first draft of every novel is hand written.

She has been a Christian for more than half her life. She goes to Carey Baptist where she is one of four registrars.

She can be found all over the net.

Website – www.revell124.plus.com/clarerevell

Facebook - clarerevellauthor

She is also on twitter and Instagram as Clare Revell.

Other books by Clare Revell

CHRISTMAS
Season for Miracles
Saving Christmas
Times Arrow
An Aussie Christmas Angel
Fairytale of Headley Cross
Christmas Eva
A Mummy for Christmas
Down in Yon Forest
The Hector Clause
Once Upon A Christmas – Dec 2017

NOVELLAS
Cassie's Wedding Dress
Carnations in January Flowers Can Be Fatal #1
Violets in February Flowers Can Be Fatal #2
Daffodils in March Flowers Can Be Fatal #3
Sweet peas in April Flowers Can Be Fatal #4
Lily of the Valley in May Flowers Can Be Fatal #5
Roses in June Flowers Can Be Fatal #6
Water lilies in July Flowers Can Be Fatal #7
Gladioli in August Flowers Can Be Fatal #8
Forget-me-nots in September Flowers Can Be Fatal #9
Marigolds in October Flowers Can Be Fatal #10
'Mums in November Flowers Can Be Fatal #11

Holly in December Flowers Can Be Fatal #12
Zara's Folly – July 2017
Quinn's Choice – Dec 2017
Xavier's Redemption – summer 2018
Married by Easter – Ash Wednesday 2018

NOVELS
After The Fire
Monday's Child Monday's Child Series #1
Tuesday's Child Monday's Child Series #2
Wednesday's Child Monday's Child Series #3
Thursday's Child Monday's Child Series #4
Friday's Child Monday's Child Series #5
Saturday's Child Monday's Child Series #6
Sunday's Child Monday's Child Series #7
Turned
Dark Lake – coming soon – Signal Me sequel

FREE READS
Kisses from Heaven
Shadows of the Past (Times Arrow Sequel)
Dutch Crocus (flowers can be fatal series finale)

PASSPORT TO ROMANCE
Vegas Vacation
Welsh Wildfire

PURE AMORE
Battle of the Flowers
Keepsake

All That Glitters

YOUNG ADULT NOVELS
November Charlie Signal Me #1
Delta Victor Signal Me #2
Echo Foxtrot Signal Me #3

ANTHOLOGIES
Red (anthology of devotions)
Cooking with Grace (anthology of recipes)
I Thirst (anthology of devotions)

Her books can be found –
Amazon UK
Amazon US
Pelican Book Group

Printed in Great Britain
by Amazon